CARNIVAL IN TRINIDAD AND OTHER STORIES

The first story in this collection of short stories is told by a man who decides to murder his freeloading business partner, Christopher Fairfax. A junior partner in his company, Fairfax was sent to work in their Trinidad practice, where he was made a senior partner for tax purposes. There, he lived on company money — even charging them for his drinks. Fairfax's partner decided that the annual carnival — with its accompanying loud music and laughter — would be the perfect time to dispose of him.

TERENCE KELLY

CARNIVAL IN TRINIDAD
and other stories

Complete and Unabridged

ULVERSCROFT
Leicester

First Large Print Edition
published 2001

British Library CIP Data

Kelly, Terence, *1920 –*
    Carnival in Trinidad and other stories.—Large print ed.—
    Ulverscroft large print series: general fiction
    1. Large type books
    I. Title
    823.9′14 [F]

    ISBN 0–7089–4374–8

Published by
F. A. Thorpe (Publishing)
Anstey, Leicestershire

Set by Words & Graphics Ltd.
Anstey, Leicestershire
Printed and bound in Great Britain by
T. J. International Ltd., Padstow, Cornwall

This book is printed on acid-free paper

Contents

Carnival in Trinidad

Christopher Fairfax had been my partner for about two years by the time I decided the only solution was to kill him. It is difficult now to remember when it was it first occurred to me that there was no alternative, but I think it was probably at the Andersons' cocktail party when he was invited to stay with the select few for dinner and I was not. That may seem a small reason for wanting to kill someone, and, of course, if it had only been incidents like that I should never have had the idea at all. But the affront was symptomatic of all that had happened since he had first come out from England to take over the Trinidad practice. In the old days, in London, when Fairfax really had been a junior partner, I had been very close to the Andersons, so much so that they used to give little dinner-parties in my honour whenever I came out to get away from the English winter for a month or two. Now they did not even bother to issue their invitations directly but added them like postscripts — when they thought of it at all — at the end of their interminable, chatty conversations with Fairfax, and he would relay the message in his bluff, hearty, spurious voice while his eyes across the office desk discouraged my acceptance. I never knew whether the discouragement was double-think, because he always seemed to have an insight into the way I would react and there was nothing that gratified him more than to be the presence at a party to which I came on sufferance.

You may wonder why I promoted him from junior partner in London to senior partner in Trinidad. The answer is, I did no such thing. It was Her Majesty's Inland Revenue which promoted him. The law relating to overseas partnerships is very simple. As long as you leave the profits overseas and make no attempt to participate in control or management of the business, the Government is happy to whistle for its share of tax. I don't like lawyers, but they have their uses, and I always do what they advise. And so Mr Christopher Bingham Fairfax was elevated when I decided to hive Trinidad off and make it a separate affair. I can remember as if it were yesterday the diffident way in which he accepted the suggestion. It wasn't that he cared for the responsibility, but if it was a good thing for me and for the firm then he was prepared to shoulder it — and I remember the firm handclasp and the true blue of his eyes as he took his copy of the document.

It's a funny thing how someone can work for you in the same office and you can see him every day for ten years and still be hoodwinked as to the man he really is, and yet in half a dozen letters, when he is five thousand miles away, you can read his substance. I think I liked him then, when he was in England. It's all so clouded now that I find it difficult to remember, but the way I liked him was not the way the Andersons and all the others came to like him. I liked him in the way a builder likes his foreman, so that we always had an easy camaraderie that ended when the door had closed. It was always Fairfax on one side and Mister on the other, and I think that was the first thing in his letters which provoked me — when he dropped the Mister.

Even so, it would not have signified, none of it, if things had gone on the way they always had, with London all-important and Trinidad a trifling enterprise.

Now Trinidad is paramount. I won't say Fairfax made no contribution, but he did not have to start as I did, years ago, unknown: he built on a foundation, a foundation I had laid. People have short memories. I wonder how soon they will forget Fairfax now that he is dead.

I spoke of the Andersons — but there was much more in it than just that. There was the financial aspect. Things fell apart in London when we had the credit squeeze. But it didn't work out like that out here. When I remember how he used to thank me for his bonus, and after only a year in Trinidad he had the *Financial Times* sent out from England and spent an hour every morning working out how much more money he had made . . . I wonder how long it will be before someone thinks to cancel that damned pink paper. Thank God I won't have to watch him push aside the morning post in that irritating way he had, and cut the string, and fold and unfold it, this way and that, casually, as if it were of no importance what the figures said, when it was all he thought about, morning, noon and night, money — and how long it would be before he could leave the tropics and buy that house on the golf course he was always boasting he was going to have. That's how he saw himself . . . a suburban squire. He wasn't very good at golf. I could always beat him, but just the same they'd have made him captain in a year or two. He had the manner, he'd taken care to cultivate it. It was all there. The pipe and the big smile and the belly laugh. That damned laugh. You couldn't be in the same room with him without having it rammed down your throat every few minutes, and the other fools used to laugh with him, and they'd all be standing around in a group laughing their stupid heads off at some inane remark he'd made. It was just like that at the Andersons the night I knew I couldn't stand it any longer. I'd have sent him packing back to England, there and then, if the agreement would have let me. But I couldn't. The Inland Revenue and the lawyers and Mr. Christopher Fairfax had seen to that. There was nothing I could do, nothing. My own business and I couldn't buy a twopenny stamp unless I got him to agree. The staff knew how it was. I could see it from their silly, supercilious faces whenever I made suggestions. They'd give me lip service and no sooner had I gone than they'd be back doing it the way he'd told them to. They knew how it was all right, they knew that I couldn't do anything except draw my share of profit. But they didn't know the way he used to milk the business so that the profits were ridiculous. He had a name for generosity. In two years he never bought a drink that wasn't paid by me. My God, when I think back on it. The clubs and the cars and the petrol and the restaurant accounts. He used to say it was good for trade. Like that last party he gave on the day of Carnival. He took the best suite overlooking the Savannah; the one with the balcony which stretches all along its length. And he had them fix a bar so that everyone could help themselves. Everyone. Not just the Andersons and people like that, but everyone. The hangers-on and the waifs and strays and the inebriates and anyone who happened to pass the door

But I didn't mind then. Not that day. Not that day because it was his last. I knew that night at the Andersons' I would kill him on the day of Carnival. The second day of Carnival if I am to be precise. Perhaps I ought to tell you something about Carnival in Trinidad or you won't really understand why it should be so perfect. But I can't describe it well enough. Not so that you could know what Carnival is really like. You have to be there in the streets, amongst the people, with the steel bands and the shuffling feet and the sizzling heat and the costumes, the fantastic costumes. It's not any one of these things, it's all of them and more. It's not just the performers, the shuffling thousands punch drunk with the beat of a thousand pans, it's the spectators who aren't spectators but part of Carnival. It's not like the Lord Mayor's Show with Floats as isolated incidents and the people lining the streets good-mannered and good-humoured with a policeman here and there to keep it nice and tidy. That's just what Carnival isn't. It's got its parts but the parts aren't isolated, they're blended like fine brandy. And Carnival in Trinidad doesn't just occur like the Lord Mayor's Show occurs. It builds up. It starts when Port of Spain and San Fernando and Arima start jumping-up weeks before. And it creeps into you, the beat and the steel pans and the excitement. I've seen it happen. I've seen the judges and the lawyers looking down their Roman noses when the jump-up starts; and I've seen them at the Country Club when Carnival is dying, jumping-up with a little stick between their palms and their eyes closed and the sweat running down their faces. I've seen the girls holding the stick with its end pressed into their navels and their bodies swaying and the pans and the kettles and the brake-drums thumping. I know what it's like at Jou Ouvert when the cocks crow on Monday and the bands start collecting at Santa Cruz and Maraval and at Curepe and march their way into Port of Spain. I've seen the people gather in the streets, the blacks and the whites and the in-betweens and the Indians and the Chinese and the Africans. They gather and they crowd and they follow the bands. They

7

spill from the pavements into the gutters, and they shuffle so that you can hear the thud and the shuffle and the tramp of a thousand feet echoing up right through Monday into Tuesday when the big bands form. Not just scores but hundreds, maybe thousands. And all in masquerade. Kings, queens, soldiers, sailors, Saracens, Crusaders, Ethiopians, Assyrians, Egyptians, witch-doctors, savages, thieves and murderers. Red, blue, gold, yellow, white, pink, puce, ebony. Swords, daggers, armour, lace, shields, cutlasses, visors, helmets. Glistening black bodies, head-dresses, tunics and skirts and tattered jeans. I've watched them as they march A hundred Vikings and a score of drums and the shuffling shuffling feet and the swaying sweating bodies, and five hundred Seabees drab green beneath the cruel sun, and then Atlantis with flying banners and ostrich plumes and blood-red cloaks lined in gold, frosted breastplates over turquoise habits embroidered in strange arabesques, wild eyes, black faces, silver helmets and a hundred spears waving to the poignant, sad and strident wave of sound, and the people mingling, pulsing, shuffling, dancing, singing, shouting and moving with the stream.

I've seen it in the hotels with all order

8

gone, with the public rooms cluttered and the bar packed like matches in a box, with jump-up in the foyer and rowdy parties everywhere. There are no parts in Carnival that can be separated and Carnival isn't here or there. It's in the hotels as it is in the streets or on the green Savannah, and there is laughter and singing and jumping-up and the sounds of drums. There are sleepers lying anywhere and drunkards comatose. There are sudden shrieks and falling bodies. There could be no better time for murder.

The door was open, jammed with a wedge so that they could see he had no enemies. Come in and be my guest. Take a glass and empty out the drink that someone left unfinished and fill it up and meet my friends out here on the balcony, the biggest balcony in Port of Spain. You know the Andersons, of course, and Edgar? Look, there's Sir Archibald, down there and to the left. It's very kind of you, I'll come if I have time. I'm going home on leave in May, we'll meet in Verreys. No shop today.

Who's that? Why that's my partner. I go across out of obscurity. I didn't know you had a partner, Chris. I am dismissed or just forgotten.

The tablecloth is stained with rum and Scotch and burnt with stubs from cigarettes,

9

and the bottles are in disarray amongst the dirty glasses.

I empty something into gin or water and swill the glass with tonic and fill it up again. My body seems to soak the spirit into it as if it had no stomach.

I can feel the shape of the knife inside my pocket, see it as if I held it in my hand. It is a very cheap affair, a piece of metal stuffed into a wooden hilt. A plain deal wooden hilt. They sell them for the fishermen to cut their lines and slit the throats of fish. It has a little scabbard. A tawdry piece of leather, roughly sewn, and around the handle a thin strip with a press-stud like they have on gloves. A knife too cheap to save, too commonplace to claim.

The people come and go and drink my drinks and smoke my cigarettes and thank my partner for his hospitality. The perfect squire upon his balcony.

He comes across the room but someone calls him back and he laughs, a belly laugh. He takes his pipe and fills it in his mouth, grinning his aimiable fatuous grin along its length. His fingers work the tobacco into the bowl and when it is full search for his matches in his pocket, but the true blue eyes are steady as they always are. Another group comes bursting through, shouting to him from the doorway, and squeeze their way on to the balcony, drawing his attention to something down below and all of them lean over calling to someone underneath. He clasps his fists together above his shoulder and shakes them in the manner of a boxer before the fight begins. And then they all troop out, brushing past me as they go, and leaving me alone with the debris and the stale sweat and smoke.

The noise of the steel bands marching through sweeps in as if their voices had formed a barrier now removed, and I go on to the balcony and look down at the street narrowed by the teeming, jogging mass into a narrow strip. Ahead, a vast contingent of Marines, their helmets camouflaged as if for jungle warfare, their wooden rifles ported, have broken ranks and prance and jog and sway into the Savannah. Behind, a forest of thin lances, picked-out with yellow pennons, flashes the sun and jigs up and down presaging some historical facsimile and attracts the crowd which lifts itself up on tiptoe, and in front, a pasticcio of individual players mime people of strange times and places. A witch-doctor, with a head-dress ten feet high and eight feet wide yoked around his neck, a gaudy patchwork of white, red and yellow plumes with horns of brilliant blue and a crown and dress of gold, dances savagely, mocking a bishop in pearls and white with cope and shepherd's crook; a knight in armour, with a purple cloak and a shield quartered in red and orange and emblazoned with an eagle, feints with his staff towards the Queen of Zanzibar.

I could go into the streets and stand amongst the crowd and let the pans drum out my rancour while there's time. I could take my petty hatred and drown it in a sea of sound and sweat until there's only my feet and fingers, hands and toes and hips and head moving to the insistent beat that's over Trinidad. I could be there with the rest of them, jumping-up, until the rum pours from my body in the heat, and envy, pride and malice are words that I have never heard.

I turn towards the door, decided, but decision comes too late, for the whole gang with throats parched from screeching, heads towards the room and blunders through the door and Carnival retreats until it's just an exhibition like the Lord Mayor's Show. The belly laughs are back and the drums are gone and patience comes to aid my resolution. I pour another drink and wait and listen.

I said that it was strange how a man could be anonymous although you thought you knew him. It's just as strange how when that anonymity has gone at last, you can feel his thoughts as if they were your own or, even more than that, how you can understand him as he cannot understand himself.

It was like that when he came over.

I could tell he was aware there was something that was not as it should be on the day of Carnival. When he felt unsure his *bonhomie* would swell like the stupid puffer fish which blows itself up to enormous size at hint of danger. He talked of business and spoke in cliches. He said the ground was laid, the seeds were sown; from now on we would reap. He wiped the grin away and replaced it with his business look, made openings for me to speak, listened with gravity to what I had to say, and nodded in agreement as if I had explained away his problem. We'll talk about it after Carnival, he said, as if we had disposed of what we had to say and he could return to the balcony with menace exorcised. There's just one thing, I said. What's that? Not here.

He shrugged his shoulders and left the room with me. He did not even think to say goodbye. They never even saw him go.

The hall was emptyish. A girl and a man cuddling in a corner; a lift attendant who had shirked his chores talking to a maid. The staircase was nearby. There were three floors below us. Six flights. Fifty, sixty, steps, I thought. He went ahead holding his pipe to his mouth with one hand, the other sliding down the hand-rail. I took the knife from my pocket, the pocket of my bushcoat, and slid it gently into the pocket of my trousers. I could feel the touch of wood against my fingers and with every step the movement of the muscles of my thigh against my palm. I looked to see what hint the knife would give, and saw the crease that ran from my knuckles to its point, and watched the way my trousers bellied to the knee and straightened with every step I took. I used the second flight to synchronize our steps so that when the time came I would find the spot as I had practised in my bedroom. He was taller than I or it might have been impossible. I watched his shoulders carefully and the way his hips swung a little with every step he took. You can spend a lifetime and never know the way a man walks down a staircase, and then in a dozen stairs you can know how every muscle works. I watched the way he took a firmer grip to swing himself around the inside of the staircase on the second floor, the way he left his hand behind so that mine sliding down almost touched it and then the way he swept it forward ahead of him. There was no one on the second floor and there'd be no one on the floor below because the canopy cut off the

14

view from the bedrooms there. I would have liked to kill him so that he would have stumbled down the final flight into the crowd in the foyer, but it would have been a ridiculous thing just for the moment's pleasure. The place was on the landing between the first and second floors. I listened, but there were only the more distant sounds. There was nothing on the first and second floors and going higher they would use the lift.

I watched his foot reach for its last step but one and took the knife from my pocket openly and raised it up until it was at the level it had to be, and I ran my hand ahead of me and grasped the rail and pulled my body forward. I felt the pressure of my toes against the stairs and concentrated on the spot I had to strike. He had one step to take and I one thrust and only one. His foot reached for the landing and mine pressed hard against the stair, and I took the knife as firmly as I could and launched myself upon his back and saw the colour and the pattern of his shirt and then my wrist and palm were tight up hard against it. I knew I had struck it where I should and I pulled backwards and sideways on the hilt and the loosened blade remained inside him as I had intended.

I had no feelings as I saw him fall,

sprawling his way and sliding down the stairs, but I heard his pipe rattling ahead of him and saw it bounce clear on to the hall before I turned away and went back up the stairs. I went into the toilet and took the tissues from my pocket and wiped my hand and cleaned the handle of the knife, and then I flushed the tissues out of sight and dropped the handle down the letter chute outside, and walked through the open door and back into the room.

It seemed a long time to be standing there wondering how soon they would find him and whether I should go to the balcony so that they would know that I was in the room, but Anderson came over to fill his glass and make his duty call. We talked banalities until the conversation died. Where's Chris? he said. I've no idea, he left ten minutes back. He nodded and went back to the balcony. I followed him. It didn't matter now to go across and join them. I leaned over the rail and looked into the street. There was a hint of evening in the sky. I was perturbed by the void where feelings should have been. There was no relief nor fear nor triumph. Not even apprehension. It was as if it had not happened, as if below there was no curious mob goggling at what was left of him, no body leaking blood. I thought of why I'd killed him and now the reasons seemed as small as the fact that he was dead. I wondered if he'd finished on his back or on his face. If on his back they'd think he was another drunk and all walk round him grinning; but if he'd finished on his face there'd be an inch of knife protruding and they'd know, and then they'd be asking how on earth you found a policeman in the midst of Carnival and there wouldn't be anyone who'd want to lose the sense of holiday and they would be irritated that he had to choose so unfortunate a time to be a murderer's victim. They'd call the manager as if it were his business and he'd come over, pushing through the scrum, cursing the inconvenience of it and calculating its effect, and then they'd call the police who would have to fight their way up through the crowds. I could imagine the police car honking and hooting and the people jumping-up in front of it, and all around it, thinking it was part of Carnival, and the constables and the detectives deserting it despairingly and pushing, shoving, prising their way through the mass — so that by the time they arrived there wouldn't be a single person who could really say how long it was since they had found the body. I realised that I would have to see them and I visualised the Inspector with his peaked cap and his baton and his putteed legs, elbowing his way, and I think it was then I felt the first emotion. What was so odd about it was that I felt exactly as I had at school when they had dared me to commit a schoolboy crime and I had done so and they had all lost interest and the punishment was bitter in my mouth. I could sense the fear creeping and crawling and I sought to summon up my loathing as an ally, but I could not picture him, only the patterning of his shirt and the hollow firmness of his back where my palm had struck it and I could not hear his laugh, only the skittering of his pipe ahead of him. I could remember nothing of what it was that had made me hate him, I could only remember the sickening thud of his face upon the stairs and the way he slithered downwards with his body jiggling over every tread. There was nothing of him when he lived that I could call to mind and nothing to offset the dismal qualms which came by stealth and filled the void where exultation should have been.

The fear came like a mist that steals over the fields beside a river-bank, cold and dank and white, smothering warmth, obliterating everything except itself, and I knew that if I did not crush it it would take command so that they would only need to look at me to know that I had killed him. So I gazed into the street and tried to lose myself in Carnival. Races of Africa they called themselves, the band that stretched from Frederick Street to the Savannah. Zulus, Fuzzy-wuzzys, Congolese, mysterious Arabs dressed in flowing white, and Negroes with leopard skins around their loins, pygmy women, Sudanese, and skinny natives from the Western Coast, tarbooshed Egyptians, Ethiopians with beards. Assegais and blowpipes, spears and daggers. Necklaces and charms and ju-jus by the score and savage rites and dances all along. And yet it seemed to me no more than an exhibition, and the chanting voices were without effect; my feet were still, and I thought that perhaps in the whole of Port of Spain I was the only one who stood outside of Carnival. There was nothing there in the street below to rid me of the fear which held me rigid, waiting for the feet outside the door, the shouts, the questions. The strength that should have come from malice was gone with my capacity to ressurect the chafing anger which had made me murder him and I stood weak and silent knowing my fear would sentence me as I had sentenced him.

I was the only silent one, and I could hear them jabbering as I heard the chanting of the band below, and nothing that they said touched me until someone talked of him.

This party's flat, where's Chris? some idiot said, and all at once the loathing overflowed and swept away in an instant the mists of fear and I knew that I could face the questioners because it needed only for them to use his name, as they would always have to, to make the reasons for his killing ample.

And I was right, for when the first of them came rushing in, his eyes aglow with the excitement of his news, I could listen with the rest of them with narrowed eyes and open mouth and I could make the same remarks. Who could it be, I don't believe it, only a madman would do such a thing. And I could race down those same stairs with them to view his corpse, cursing the gabbling, jabbering, gibbering crowd around him, levering my way through them as my right as partner gave me and kneeling at his side in the way they all expected.

He had ended on his face and there was an inch of knife, but I couldn't see his pipe amongst the feet around me.

The policemen came at last. I don't suppose now I come to think of it they would have come in from the front, but it doesn't matter any more than it matters that the Inspector was without puttees although he held a baton. They had no trouble keeping back the mob, there is a strange timidity that sets a proper distance from a body, but outside this perimeter the crowd swelled as the news was spread and the lift was going up and down until there were as many on the flight of stairs above as that below and Christopher Bingham Fairfax held his last court with his feet pointing to the sky and his head wedged between the landing and the bottom step and an inch of knife protruding from his back. He liked to be with people when he lived, but he had his largest audience now. I think he would have liked it if he'd known.

We went upstairs, the policemen and the manager and the Andersons and the rest of us, and they cordoned off the stairs and put a guard upon the lift, and the small ingredients of Carnival the murder had disturbed resumed their course. We had to wait a little longer in the third-floor room but not for long, for all of us had been together at the time and one does not bite the hand that feeds one; and down below Carnival would be streaming in and out of the hotel foyer, trampling the clues and swallowing up his murderer. Later, when Carnival was dead, we'd have a longer talk to see if there was anything that would point towards the slayer of a man who had no enemies; meanwhile the living lived, the bands were in the streets, the climax of the day had yet to come.

I felt for them, struggling for the formula that would express a decent grief but would not pack them off to bed. It must be difficult when your host is dead to carry on as if he were alive, but fortunately they had the air of Carnival to give them sustenance and then again I needed their support. There's nothing you can do, you know, you've got to carry on, they said. We'll stick with you and see it through. You can't stay moping in a hotel bedroom, and if you do we'll come and drag you out. There was a solemn rite, drinking the health of the dear departed — and then a bill to sign. I waved aside their feeble protestations. He was my partner, it's the least that I can do. They nodded sagely and we left together.

The Country Club is where you go to dine, to drink, to dance, at the end of Carnival. Of course it isn't dancing as you know it, it's jumping-up, with or without a stick. I prefer a stick held between my palms and I like to close my eyes and let the music drown me, and best of all I like to be as close as I can to the band itself. I could stay on the same square yard of floor for the whole of the evening hearing the shuff shuff of the feet keeping time, feeling the point of the stick against my palms with the whole of my body moving to the beat. I never knew till jump-up that you can be like this, use every muscle of your body and yet be stationary, feel music taking hold of you until there is nothing but you and the beat and the sweat pouring down your face. Of course you can't stay there up against the band because that's what the others want to do, the men in their hot shirts and the women in their jeans and slacks and anything they thought to wear, they all want to be there because they feel the same as you. If you didn't know, if you came suddenly out of the cold of England into the heat of the night you'd hear the beat and you'd wonder what it was and then when you saw their faces and their little sticks and the way they moved without moving and the hot shirts on their backs, you'd think it was the rum but it isn't that at all. The rum or the whisky or the beer has nothing to do with it and it isn't even the music or the bands or the tropical night, it's simply Carnival in Trinidad and there isn't any other explanation. It doesn't matter that your host got murdered, or you killed your partner, that sort of thing is just an incident once the jump-up has really taken hold of you, so after the first hour or so while the Country Club filled and the band warmed up, the Andersons and the others forgot him. But I did not. I could stand there, swaying to the music and feeling my heels lifting and my shoulders jigging, and I could think about him and think what it would have been like if I hadn't killed him and he'd been there on the floor with his vast good nature and his perpetual smile, and I could think what it was like now to be alive and hot, listening to the beat and watching the people, instead of being stiff and dead and quite forgotten.

But nothing goes on for ever, and Carnival ends at midnight and then everyone at the Country Club goes down to the swimming-pool and people start jumping in with all their clothes on, or they get thrown in with all their clothes on, and the pool fills up like you never normally see it filled because no one wants to let go, and they hang on just like a child brings back a bucket of sand and a crab from his holidays, but even that has to come to an end and when it did there was Anderson ready to take me back. I don't know what had happened to his wife, perhaps they'd thrown her in the pool and she was somewhere wringing out her clothes and suddenly remembering that her Chris wasn't there any more to flirt with and to hang on to and feeling too ashamed to face me. Anyway, there was Anderson ready to take me back to my hotel because I didn't have a car, looking a little shamefaced himself and reminding me that it was too early to forget.

I was not surprised when he suggested we had a nightcap in my room, it's the kind of thing you can forecast, but what did surprise me was that there was a message that the Inspector would be coming back to see me. It wasn't that I was worried, I knew there could be no evidence to link me with his death even if they had found the hilt, but I was surprised that he could not wait until the morning, but I suppose he had his reasons.

Anderson was very quiet as if he had used up all he had to say at jump-up but I didn't fill it in. It was his idea to stay and all I wanted was to go to bed and work out what I had to do about the Trinidad office now that I hadn't got a partner to run it for me, that and think about killing Fairfax, in case it never felt so good again.

Anderson got round to it at last. It wasn't much. At least, it wasn't much to him the way he looked at it. All he wanted to do was to talk about Fairfax, to give him an obituary, so that it all ended up nice and tidy and he could say tomorrow he'd done his best for me.

Who would have murdered him, he asked. It must have been a madman or a drunk,

Chris wasn't positive enough. I looked at him. Not positive enough? That's so, he said, he didn't have his enemies like most of us, because, you see, he had no depth. People like that are left in peace. Who is it that gets murdered? Politicians, millionaires and lovely women. People with depth of one sort or another. He hadn't any depth at all. You couldn't take him seriously. Why should you murder him? He smiled. I don't mean you. You least of all. But figuratively? He was like a bear, a clumsy bear. All that he had was written on his face. You chose ideally. You could have had a man we loathed so that we said we'll take our work elsewhere. You could have had a man to whom we all deferred, and lost your business any time he chose. But you did better. You chose a figurehead, a simple man we had to like. A labourer. It's not disloyal to talk about him like this, he said, because Chris knew it. He knew what it was he had to do, to carry on where you had stopped. Of course he had a complex and he had to prove he served a purpose. That was why he entertained the way he did. We understood, we thanked you privately but left it there. We let him feel he was our host because it was the best for him, for you, for us. He paused and there was silence and I saw the mist begin to curl again along the

26

river-bank. Yes, he said, he was a simple man, and so they'll never find his murderer. You need a motive to do that.

What will you do, he asked. I don't know, not yet. It's far too sudden. But I knew. I'd run without a partner, take the profits, have that house myself.

You had the problem anyway, he said. I raised my head. How so? He lit a cigarette. He would have told you after Carnival. He was getting married. She was very rich. He could have had his house, gone back to England. Why should he stay? This was his farewell party.

He rose to leave. You don't look very well, he said, but then it's been a dreadful shock. There can't be any other man who would want him back alive again as much as you.

He left and the room was very silent. I walked over to the mirror and looked at what I saw and then I turned away and waited for the knock.

Their First American

It started with a Christmas card from Jamaica. The Christmas card was more like a picture postcard, showing as it did the long ridges of the Blue Mountains shimmering in the midday heat and in the foreground splashes of colour which, although the Mitchells were not to know it at the time, were the blossom of yellow poui and the salmons, scarlets, plums and pinks of bougainvillea. It all looked very lovely and quite improbable.

On the bottom right hand corner in gold lettering the word *Greetings* was inscribed obliquely and on the inside fold a banal printed message with a place for signature. But overseas friends who happen to be poor correspondents are inclined to take the opportunity offered by the blank inside page behind the picture of a Christmas card to add a few words of their own, and here was no exception. There were a few lines of this and that and then the signatures again, and after that, and possibly because the message had been badly centred, a postscript. It is said that the nub of any letter is in the postscript and certainly in the case of Ann and Peter Mitchell this was so, as, but for its six words they would never even have contemplated going to Jamaica.

They arrived in Montego Bay in May, which is a month travel agents do not advise as they have heard, quite incorrectly, that in Jamaica it does nothing but rain in May, whereas in fact it can be inconceivably beautiful and even when they come, the heavy showers and the thick black threatening clouds can be charged with drama to a couple who have never known the tropics and are still young enough to have enthusiasm. And from the point of view of seeing whether it really was worthwhile opening a branch office (which was the matter of the postcard) May was as good a month as any.

They arrived exhausted from the flight, with — from an obstinate determination not to lose one shred of the adventure — no hotel booked. The hot night hit them, the hot thick night clamorous with the cicadas and the bullfrogs and the sea, redolent with new elusive scents and the mustiness of humid soil. The short sweep of road between the airport and an anonymous hotel with fireflies flickering and the moon hanging over deep mysterious hills, choked them with emotion. A black hand opening the taxi door, a brown face behind a desk, a calypso band, hard shiny patterned floor tiles, a patio against the warm white sand, the scuff of a tiny surf whispering to the friendly, still, enveloping night, fused to a single never-to-be-forgotten marquetry and then they were asleep.

When the soft dawn, shaded by the long deep hills, filtered timorously across a sea which barely stirred and stretched like a vast counterpane of wrinkled satin, Peter Mitchell bustled his wife to wakefulness with the conceit of a cicerone that having seen the wonder of a Caribbean dawn a moment or two before her he could claim the credit for it, and standing by the wide-open sliding doors with an arm outstretched announced dramatically:

'Look at it!'

And that was the moment it was decided. The office would be opened. The postscript was entirely justified.

Ann threw back the sheet, swivelled on the bed and stared with her hair a-tumble, her eyes still blinking sleep, her feet resting on the cool gay tiles, and then, just as she was in her short white nightdress and just as he was in his crumpled blue pyjamas, they walked out from the little patio onto the sharp white sand and looked about them.

And there was the American.

He stood in a startling pair of shorts, an extravaganza of molluscs on a chrome yellow background, hairy, barrel-chested, swarthy, unshaven for perhaps a week, with the bluest eyes imaginable, viewing them with interest.

'Hi,' he said.

They saw him after breakfast on the beach. They sat with him. They spent the morning with him. He was still unshaven. It appeared he worked in television. The Public Relations side of television which called for shaving twice a day, which not only made him sore but gave him such a hate for shaving that he eschewed it completely, or almost completely, when on holiday. There were other things he didn't do. He didn't smoke and he didn't drink. It is entirely out of character for men who do not shave not to drink or smoke but there it was. He did neither. He lay in the hot bright sun, his swarthiness and the mat of hair across his chest and back protecting him, and he swam in the cool blue, green and turquoise sea; that was about all he did, except to eat and send postcards to his secretary in New York telling her the water temperature, and to sleep, and now they had arrived, to talk to Ann and Peter Mitchell.

When they thought about it afterwards, they couldn't remember much of what he talked about except two things. The first was that he teased them about the English. He was by turns satirical, amusing, ironic, always good humoured, never insulting, never offensive, but still quite simply teasing them. He teased them on every subject. Traditions, wars and aeroplane engines, roads, films and motor cars, language and pronunciation. Books, television, food and customs. He built them up to knock them down, he inserted sly sideshafts in the conversation to put himself in a position of advantage from which to pick them off.

But not all the time. He was never wearying. They talked of many things but it was this that they remembered later, when they were back in England and he was back somewhere, in New York, shaved and sore and for all they knew drinking bourbon on the rocks and getting through two packs of cigarettes a day.

Although they could never manage him, not even between the two of them, they were very taken with him. They liked the staggering blue of his eyes out of his sunburnt, scrubby, unshaven face, they liked his accent, they liked the ways he had. They liked him because he liked Jamaica as much as they did, and they liked him because he took to them to the complete exclusion of any of the other guests and this was rather satisfying, particularly when considered against the background of his teasing. And there was one final reason why they liked him, perhaps the strongest reason of all, and this was the other thing they remembered afterwards.

He thought Ann wonderful.

He called her Annie.

He was in awe of Peter that he could manage such a woman in the way he did.

He drew attention to a hundred things she did: she dried Peter's back, she warned him of the sun. She fetched her own food from the buffet table, went to the bedroom for forgotten articles, used the leaky snorkel, read the paper second, waived claim for the last cigarette in the packet. She cleaned his sunglasses, oiled areas of his body he could have reached himself, carried his bits and pieces in her handbag, rinsed his swimming trunks . . .

All these things he found remarkable. He was not dissembling; he assured them there was not a single American woman all the way from Calais Maine to San Diego who would do the same. It pleased them highly and each incident he pointed out was a victory against his teasing and a spur to recount with bland offhandedness other virtues of an English wife. With a voracious appetite he listened to their catalogue of wifely obligations: Peter taking their only car while Ann managed as best she could, the slippers before the fire and the drink poured out awaiting his return from work, Ann's struggles with the S bend (which he assured them no American woman was aware existed), the early morning cup of tea . . . They racked their brains to think of others. But although it was, perhaps, a little weighted, they kept strictly to the truth — the game would not have lasted half an hour if they had launched into absurdities.

He listened with growing admiration; on not one other facet of the English way of life could they shift him from his convictions, but on this their victory was absolute. That any man could so organise his married life was fascinating, that any woman could be so subjected and thrive on it, bewildering. He respected Peter but his admiration for Ann, called Annie, was unbounded. She was the paragon of women. She could do no wrong.

★　★　★

After a few days in Montego Bay, the Mitchells left for Kingston. They went partly because their consciences insisted that far-reaching decisions are not to be taken on the basis of emotional experiences at dawn; they had discussed it gravely (toying with slivers of fried coconut and sipping rum punches on a particularly still and langorous night when the palms around them barely rustled and the sea caressed the shore like a woman's sigh) refusing to allow themselves to be influenced by any but the most material considerations. And they went because the long deep hills invited them, whispering of Shangri-Las the tourists never saw behind the first low ridge, of mountain streams where the water hissed crystal clear between the rounded boulders, of birds and butterflies, mysterious valleys which were always cool and the trees were cloaked with succulents and the liana fell in long thin lines towards an earth which never felt the sun, of the yellow flames of kerosene lighting up black faces in sudden villages, of fruits and flowers and sights and sounds that they had never heard before.

In Kingston they achieved success beyond their wildest dreams and for very simple reasons. Jamaica had bewitched them, they were young and full of laughter, they were enthusiastic, and, above all, they listened instead of laying down the law.

In a few long days they achieved far more than any of the cohorts of businessmen they saw around them uttering unimpeachable economic truths, haggling over percentages, grim-faced from purpose, grey-faced from Northern winters. They achieved far more because when they talked of Jamaica it was not of margins and C.I.F. and F.O.B. (which in fact they didn't understand at all) but of ackees and calypsoes, of the grandeur of the mountains and how the sea was like milk to bathe in, of their rolls of films, their laundry basket bought on the way to Mandeville, the green lizards with suspicious eyes puffing out the yellow sacs beneath their necks, of loggerheads and doctor birds and old men beside the road cooking their grey goat stew, of the magic of dawn rising over Kingston from behind the mountains and how they had seen the moon come apricot over the hills before the sun had set beneath the sea at Palisadoes.

They achieved far more than the dreary businessmen because they made the Jamaicans whom they met even prouder of Jamaica than they had been before, anxious to help, amused, avuncular, nostalgic for small pleasures they had come to take for granted.

And because they achieved so much and had as well a lively eagerness, before they returned to Montego Bay they saw a good deal more of Jamaica than many who had been visiting regularly for ten or twenty years.

But of course it had to end as all things end, and the time came when they returned to their first hotel in Montego Bay to catch the flight back home the following day. They were a different couple, bursting with knowledge, brimming with confidence, ready to prate and prattle from dawn to dusk on their newest love, Jamaica. And then they were rather proud to have achieved so much in so short a time. It would have been easier to have gone back home from Kingston but now, for the first time, they felt ready for the American's teasing, certain they could manage him, and so they went back to their first hotel.

But he had left.

There was an envelope addressed to 'Pete and Annie Mitchell' and inside only a cutting from a magazine.

The cutting showed a mule plodding its weary way through a desert with nothing in sight except the far horizon and some cactus. On the mule's back under a great sombrero to protect him from the blistering heat was a Mexican and in front of the mule, pulling on a rope, a woman. The original caption had been cut away but scrawled in its place were the words: 'Just like in England.'

Cut Glass

Alec and Marjorie Littlepaige had found their Shangri-La on a glittering night from the balcony of a small guest house which overlooked the harbour of St George's in Grenada — a night when the sky was a marquetry of drifting clouds in a bowl of star-filled indigo and the air was warm and scented. They had looked down on the silvered schooners drawn up in silence against the quay and then across the water to the ampitheatre of brick and shuttered houses climbing to the ridges and knew where they would end their days. And then, the holiday over, they had gone back to their house in Finchley and Alec to his job as head salesman in the fine glass and china department of Davenports in Piccadilly.

Nothing shook them from their resolve. Over the years they made the necessary arrangements and very soon after Alec had retired they were living in a bungalow drenched with mauve and white bougeanvillea, with a small garden hedged with hibiscus and a view across the harbour along the line of Grand Anse Bay to the low misty hillocks of Point Saline.

Then, after five years, Marjorie suddenly died. At first it seemed to Alec that the purpose of living had gone and he toyed with the idea of going back to Finchley where life was better organised for ageing widowers. But in the end he stayed. It hardly seemed worth the bother when, in only a little while, he would be with Marjorie again.

But his body was obstinate and after a while Alec bestirred himself to devise a plan to occupy the years of activity left to him. There was a small hotel in which he and Marjorie had enjoyed an occasional sherry and where they had struck up an acquaintanceship with the owner, Simon Robiere, and within which was a small shop with a separate doorway and window to the street in which Robiere had stocked amongst other items, china and glass for sale to tourists. But the venture had been premature, the shop had been closed and the stock packed away in tea chests, crates and boxes awaiting the advent of better days. Alec persuaded Robiere to re-open the shop and allow him to run it.

Soon the slumbering files, the old invoices, the battered suitcases and all the rest which over the years had been unceremoniously dispatched and the tea chests, crates and boxes unpacked and their contents artistically arranged. And to them Alec had added a personal contribution — a quite magnificent cut glass bowl which had been, better than any watch, his parting gift from Davenports. He made it the centre of his display, giving it pride of place all by itself on a table behind which he sat. No visitor could fail to see it, the more particularly because each morning Alec would float in it a mass of flowers picked from his hibiscus hedge, blooms of the wild variety whose colour is so rich that when the customers bent over the bowl their redness was reflected in their cheeks.

Alec became something of a character in St George's — a quiet, thoughtful, gentle man whose shop was only open in the mornings and who never pressed a sale. Local people passing by would drop in for a chat and many tourists, whose number was greater these days, hearing of him made a point of calling. Alec liked the local people, but he liked the tourists more. Mostly they were young but he had no envy of their smooth, straight limbs and sunburnt bodies — it is only those who have been unhappy through their lives who are envious of the young and Alec had been a happy man and these years were just a time of waiting. And so he liked listening to their talk and the sound of their laughter in his little shop.

Mostly they bought the usual tourist things but now and again pieces of glass or china. He was never quite sure whether to be glad or sorry when he made this kind of sale for such items were more or less irreplaceable, the wholesalers in their dreary back street London warehouses have no time for the single figurine or the trifling four of this or six of that. So, as the seasons passed, straw mats and hats came more and more to replace the china cups and porcelain gave way to plastic in a myriad forms. There were key rings linked to plastic tabs cunningly moulded around minute sea horses and coral fragments, and there were paperweights, penholders and long slim swords with plastic hilts for opening letters. There were little boxes lined with felt their surfaces thickly patterned with tiny shells and ten inch crocodiles whose gaping mouths were painted scarlet and whose eyes were glass. There was lignum vitae and bamboo and purple heart, and there were porcupine fish, square in shape and with their skin blown out like balloons of parchment for use as lampshades. There were ropes of beads in almost every shade, and bongo drums and napkins crudely embroidered with native fruits and figures. There were many things.

The time came when the last set of tumblers and the last figurine was sold and only Alec's tranquil personality and the cut glass bowl with its floating hibiscus blooms characterized the shop from all the other tourist shops scattered throughout the small islands of the Caribbean. Often he would be asked to sell it but he would always shake his head and with a smile tell the customer that it enabled him to have his garden with him through the day and, if there was response, Alec might run his hands over the cool, cut sides and tell the story of his working life and how for more than forty years he had been custodian of a treasure house. And when the customer had gone, he might leave his hands around the cut glass bowl and let the thoughts of Marjorie and Davenports come tumbling back.

Once a month Alec would have a meeting with Robiere in the little bar with the striped Regency wallpaper whose bow window overlooked the roofs stepping down to the waterside and they would discuss the stock and possible replacements, and on one such morning Alec was about to close up for the day when the street door was pushed open by a man so tall in relation to the girl with him that she was able to pass under his arm without so much as a bob of her pretty head.

'Good morning,' Alec said, still seated, smiling up at them.

'Good morning, Sir,' the man, who spoke with a Southern drawl, said very respectfully from his enormous height. 'My wife and I . . . ' and he paused to bestow a glance of immense affection on the tiny creature at his side, ' . . . my wife and I are on our honeymoon and we would like a souvenir of Grenada to take back with us.'

'Where are you from?' said Alec.

'We're from Dallas, Tex. Texas that is . . . '

'Where the oil comes from.'

'Right!' The Texan grinned. 'Got my own well in my own back yard.'

'That must be very convenient,' Alec said, smiling — and was pleased to hear his little shop filled with laughter.

'I can show you some straw mats or coasters,' he suggested. 'They might be very useful for barbecues.'

The girl shook her head. 'We already have some, Sir.'

'A laundry basket?'

'We've got one of those as well.'

'You see, Sir,' the Texan said, 'we've been all round the islands and mostly they've got much the same to sell.' He chuckled deeply. 'I guess we've got so many mats and so much linen we could furnish *two* apartments. But we like Grenada best of all and we'd like to buy something to remind us especially of it.'

Alec scratched his head. 'There's nothing,' he said, 'very special in Grenada. Why don't you just browse around and see if there's anything that takes your fancy. And don't worry if there isn't, there's absolutely no obligation to buy.'

'We don't want to waste your time, Sir,' said the girl.

Alec looked at her. She was as pretty as paint with brown bare shoulders and in a yellow sun dress. He thought that if he and Marjorie had had a daughter they'd have been content if she'd been just like her.

'My dear,' he said, 'I have plenty of time. There's no hurry. Just browse around and see if there's anything you like.'

He watched them as they moved around his shop, picking things up and putting them down again. It was obvious there was nothing that they wanted. He heard a whispered conversation and then the girl came across holding a conch shell.

'I guess we'll take this,' she said.

'You don't really want it, do you?' Alec said. 'You've got one already, haven't you?'

'We've got three,' the girl said and her chuckle warmed him. 'But we've taken up so much of your time.'

'No,' said Alec. 'You've given me so much of yours.'

44

The girl looked at him. 'Gee,' she said, 'that's the sweetest thing I ever heard.'

And the man came across and, putting his arm around his wife's tiny waist, said:

'And that goes for me too, Sir.'

And as Alec, a little embarrassed, glowed with pleasure, the girl said firmly:

'Chuck — I'm not leaving this shop until we find something we want and when we get back home we'll put it somewhere where we can always see it, and if either of us gets crabby . . .'

And she could say no more.

The man patted her, like a gentle bear. 'Sure, honey, sure,' he said. 'We'll find something.'

'I think I know what you might like,' Alec said quietly. 'This bowl.'

He would have liked to have held it aloft but it was far too heavy for him so he simply put his hands around it and enjoyed the feel of the cool ridges and valleys.

'Gee, Chuck, that's swell,' the girl said and as she buried her face in the flowers thinking there might be scent in them, her cheeks were turned to flame.

The Texan was looking at Alec, trying to read his face. 'Is it really for sale, Sir?' he said. 'I mean — your shop wouldn't look the same without it.'

'Of course it's for sale,' Alec said defiantly. 'Everything in here is for sale.'

'It's such a pity to take the flowers out,' the girl said. 'They look so beautiful.'

'I shall have to take them out anyway,' said Alec. 'I always shut at lunchtime and they won't last until tomorrow. Hibiscus only lasts a day, you know.' And he stood and coming round the table took one of the blooms and she stood quite still while he threaded it into her hair over her ear. 'There,' he said. 'You look very lovely.' And, leaving her, he started to take the flowers from out of the bowl and put them in a cardboard box. 'If you'd like to take it,' he said while he was doing this, 'it'll cost you twenty dollars.'

'Twenty . . . only twenty dollars?'

'Twenty dollars,' Alec said. 'Will you take it?'

'Why sure we will..' the man began, but Alec stopped him.

'I'm afraid it's rather heavy for me. Perhaps you'll empty the water in the street, will you?'

The Texan shook his head but, taking the bowl, went out into the blazing street and poured the water into the gutter. When he came back, Alec was already making a space in another cardboard box packed with straw. Then he took back the bowl and placing it in the box let his fingers play on its sides for a few moments. But when he had finished the packing his hands were as businesslike as his voice had been.

★ ★ ★

When the couple had gone, Alec locked up his shop and made his way to the hotel bar.

'You're late today, man,' said Robiere.

'I had a very busy morning,' Alec said, accepting his sherry.

'Good,' said Robiere. 'Good. I've been thinking about the stock. You remember those pretty pottery earrings that girl showed us some samples of . . . '

Alec, sipping his sherry, let him go on — he was thinking about the red hibiscus in the young girl's hair.

'Simon,' he said after a while, interrupting. 'I just sold the cut glass bowl.'

Robiere was astonished. 'But you said you'd never sell it, man!'

Alec finished his sherry.

'I know I did,' he said. 'We say a lot of things.' He stood. 'I won't bother with lunch today. I think I'll go straight up to the house.' He crossed to the door, then paused, hand on the knob.

'By the way,' he said. 'I think you ought to

start looking for someone else to run the shop.'

'But, Alec . . . '

Alec smiled.

'I'm getting too old for it,' he said. 'Losing my touch.'

'But where,' said Robiere — but really only because he wondered how Alec would fill his time with no shop to run — 'can I possibly find a salesman as good as you — someone with so many years' experience?'

'Too much experience,' Alec said. 'I'm afraid I'm not a good salesman any more. That bowl — I'm afraid they only gave me twenty dollars for it.'

And he went out into the street and began the slow climb to his home above the harbour. And he had forgotten the bowl already — his thoughts were only filled with Marjorie.

Ashes:

A Trilogy

Cecil

Every golf club has such a member. He is overeager, garrulous and too ready to advise. His memory is prodigious — he can recall, and frequently does recall, the classic moments in his golfing life: that thirty-five yard putt he sunk, that chip which saved the day. He will tell you the best clubs to buy, the longest ball, how high to set your tee, which iron to use. He is usually a dreadful golfer.

On the other hand he is desperately keen, extraordinarily resilient and generous to a fault. If you claim a scrape he will agree unhesitatingly and offer you casual water on the least pretext. He will never query your card nor fiddle his own, never stumble his ball to a better lie in the rough. He is liberal in his praise, sympathetic when you fluff, ever ready with an excuse on your behalf.

When partners are being drawn you keep your fingers crossed in the hope that someone else will get him and when they do you are ashamed for you know he is at heart a decent fellow and that his verbosity and irritating knowledgeability spring from insecurity and an ever reborn hope of achieving something he has never yet achieved, and never will achieve, a reasonable round of golf.

* * *

Cecil was such a man. Golf was his life. He took all the magazines, read all the books and practised putting by the hour into a curious contraption in his sitting-room. Bright and early, rain or shine, he made himself available in the locker room every Saturday and Sunday morning. Easily the worst golfer in the club, he served as a kind of makeweight in extremis. Until one morning!

* * *

Walter strode into the locker room. ''morning Mac, 'morning Leslie. Sorry I'm late.'

'Where's Gordon?' Mac demanded — for Walter and Gordon normally came together.

'He isn't coming?'

'What are ye saying, man!' cried Mac incredulously.

'Is he ill?' said Leslie.

Walter shook his head. 'He's given it up.'

'What!', said Leslie, disbelieving.

'Get away wi' ye!' said Mac.

'It's Joanna,' Walter explained. 'She's given him an ultimatum. Golf or her.'

'But she can't!' said Leslie anguished. 'Not after twenty years.'

'Well she has. We'll have to find another fourth.'

* * *

Which was how it came about that Cecil played with them. He was pretending to be cleaning his clubs, hoping against hope someone would ask him to make up. He had to have overheard their conversation.

'Better ask Cecil, I suppose,' suggested Walter in an undertone.

'All that blather,' muttered Mac.

'I'll do it,' said Leslie between his teeth.

* * *

'Well, fine,' chattered Cecil who rarely played in such exalted company. 'Fine. Only too pleased to help you out. Sorry to hear about Gordon but I must say it's a bit of luck for me. I feel on song today, right bang on song. I just know it's going to be one of those mornings when I'm going to be able to string it all together . . . '

And still at it on the tee:

' . . . and I put it plumb in the middle just short of the brook and I'd have been on in two, I reckon, if I hadn't had the most wicked lie. A real cliff hanger. Even Tiger Woods . . . '

'How many did ye take?'

'Actually nine . . . But that's the way it goes. I mean that's the charm of the game, isn't it? I've forgotten what you play off Mac.'

'Eight.'

'And Leslie's three, isn't he? And you Walter?'

'Seven.'

'And I'm twenty-eight. So if we play together Leslie . . . '

★ ★ ★

Leslie drove. Two hundred and thirty yards down the middle of the fairway.

'Great shot,' said Walter.

'Pretty good, partner, pretty good,' said Cecil weighing it up. 'Pity you didn't give it a bit more air, though. With this wind you'd have got ten yards more.'

'Maybe ye'd like it back.'

'Och no man, it'll do,' said Cecil appallingly. 'Well here we go.' And, after a ferocious slice: 'Anyone see it?'

'Where d'ye think it went?'

'Well it felt all right except maybe it had a bit of draw . . . '

'A bit o' draw. Ye never got a bit of a draw

on a goff ball in yer life. I'll tell ye where it is. Right in the middle of yon flaming wood . . . '

*   *   *

As they made their way from the eighteenth green Walter, having won by eight and seven, made the grave error of thanking Cecil for the game.

'Glad to help out, Walter. Any time. If Gordon isn't back with you, how about a return next week? I must say I really did enjoy it. Might have been closer of course. You know where it went wrong, Leslie? On the third. When I put you in the trap. Mind you, you were a bit ambitious taking a seven . . . still we all make errors now and then don't we? Gosh, I'm dry. What'll you have? I'll go ahead and set them up . . . '

They watched in dismay as he strode off to the members' bar.

'He enjoyed it', said Leslie. 'Three and a half hours and not one shot that didn't make me wince . . . '

'And,' said Walter, 'so bloody grateful that we asked him.'

'And now we're stuck wi' him next week!' said Mac.

*   *   *

And so it was — *and* on the week following when Cecil suggested he switched and played with Walter. *And* on the week after that when it was, after all, only reasonable Mac should have him. Maybe they would have nipped it in the bud but they still hoped Gordon would reassert himself and twenty years of delightful Saturday and Sunday golf would be resumed. But Joanna was obdurate and by the time they faced reality, Cecil was firmly entrenched.

Each in turn had him as a partner. Each insisted it was time to make the break:

'We've got to put an end to this!'

'How?'

'Fix up wi' someone else.'

'All right. Go and fix up.'

'Well . . . well I weel.'

'And then tell him.'

'I canna . . . '

'None of us can. How can you walk out on a man who gives up all his spare time to practice so he won't let us down?'

'Or looks so bloody happy. He's blossoming!'

'Well, I dinna see why we should become permanent guid Samaritans!'

'If only he wouldn't *talk* so much . . . '

'It's no the talking I object to but the walking!'

'And the advice! Told me I wasn't cocking my wrists enough. *He* told *me!*'

'But what can we do? We're lumbered with him until we bury him! He'll stick to us like . . . like a remora!'

'Like glue!'

'Like the burrrs we pick up searching for his flaming ball!'

★   ★   ★

And so it was. They had left it too long. They had neither the heart nor the courage to make the break. The months passed. They learnt to live with the endless chatter and advice and the constant tramp into the woods to search for Cecil's golf balls. They got past the stage of irritation. They merely dreamed, as war prisoners dream, that some day they would be freed and life would recover its old, almost forgotten bliss.

★   ★   ★

There came a day when on the short thirteenth Walter and Leslie's tee shots had made the green.

'Can you split them, Mac?' said Cecil.

'Maybe.'

'What club is that.'

'It's a four.'

'You'll be short. Bound to be with this wind. I should take a three if I were you. Or even a two. You've been underclubbing all morning, Mac. So has Leslie. We're getting older, you know. Losing length. It's no good trying to force it. One gets all taut and the swing goes all to pot. Oh! Well that's a pretty good shot, I must admit. Mind you, you were a bit lucky. Wind dropped just as you hit it. Still, it's pretty good. Damn near down in one. That'll be the day won't it? When one of us does a hole in one. Thought of that since I was a kid, you know. Doing a hole in one and getting my name up on the board . . . '

'I dinna want to hurry ye, Cecil, but that fourr behind . . . '

'Sorry, Mac. But, you know. It's been a lifetime ambition. I mean . . . well, I've never said this to anyone before but I've always known I'd never be a real golfer. Get a good hole now and then. Help out occasionally. I've known inside me that was about the lot. That I'd never string nine, let alone eighteen, together. But a hole in one was always on. After all what is it? Just one good tee shot and . . . '

'Well maybe it'll be this time, Cecil. But if you don't get on with it we'll have to let them through.'

So Cecil took out his three wood and with great verve and everything about as wrong as it could be laid into his ball and hauled it round into the most tremendous hook. Even for Cecil the trajectory was remarkable and his friends (for by now they were his friends) watched its flight with mesmerised disbelief, saw it strike a tree trunk, recoil at an astounding angle towards the high bank protecting the green, bounce off it on to the green itself and running a full twenty-five yards with a marvellous borrow disappear down the hole.

Cecil stared amazed, incredulous, overjoyed.

'I've done it! I've done it! I've done it!' he cried waving his three wood in the air like a Dervish. 'I've really gone . . . and . . . done . . . it . . . '

The words died away, the three wood slipped from his hand, he stared mutely at his friends and collapsed at their feet. Walter, who was a doctor, dropped on his knees beside him, felt his pulse, looked at the other two in horrified disbelief.

'He's dead,' he said.

'Dead?'

'Dead.'

'Oh, no . . . poor old Cecil.'

'Nae, not *puir* Cecil,' said Mac.

And it was true . . . for there was a smile of perfect peace on Cecil's face.

★   ★   ★

He had left instructions. If he should happen to die before his friends in the weekend four he was to be cremated, his ashes at once collected and given to Leslie, Walter and Mac who were each to go straight to the club where one of them was to drive a ball and at the point it reached, scatter them.

It was a drear day, grey, wet and cold. Sombrely dressed in black overcoats with Walter carrying the casket and Mac a driver, they made their way to the first tee.

'Off you go, Mac,' said Walter.

'Aye.'

Mac teed up and hit a beautiful ball.

'Good shot, Mac,' said Walter, very quietly.

'Where he would have liked to have been and so seldom was,' said Leslie regretfully. 'In the middle of the fairway.'

'Let's get on wi' it,' said Mac.

They walked slowly down the fairway, three men in black not speaking until they reached the ball.

'It's never going to be the same again,' said Leslie.

'Nae,' said Mac.

'He so loved his golf,' said Walter, 'that, do you know, when they read it out that we were to do this, I suddenly felt better.'

'Aye,' Mac agreed.

'Maybe that's why he left those instructions,' said Leslie. 'To cheer us up. I don't think he'd have wanted us depressed. I think he'd have wanted to see us laughing and enjoying even a miserable afternoon like this one.'

'He talked too much and his golf was terrible,' said Walter, 'but, you know, once we'd got used to it he always made us laugh.'

'Remember that morning in the club house when we said the only time we'd be rid of him was when we buried him?'

'And I said he'd stick to us like a remora . . . '

'And I said like glue . . . '

'And I said like the burrrs we collected searching for his flaming goff ball . . . '

They fell silent, the other two watching as Walter bent, picked up the ball and handed it to Mac. Walter stood on the exact spot where it had landed, opened the casket and took out a small bag in which were all that remained of Cecil. The air was still and as they came up to him he spilled a portion of the ashes into each of their upturned palms then took the balance himself.

'Ready, Mac?' he said.

'Aye.'

'Ready, Leslie?'

'Ready.'

'All together then. One, two, three . . . throw!'

But at that moment a fierce gust of wind whipped up from nowhere, bending the trees, billowing their coat tails, and as they threw the ashes the wind blew them back and, on their black coats damp from rain, stuck, so that all three were quite covered with them and they looked at each other, stunned for a moment and then in turn each of them said:

'Like a remora.'

'Like burrrs.'

'Like glue.'

And then they smiled, then laughed. And laughed and laughed and laughed. And the wind caught their laughter and carried it across the golf course — carried it perhaps to somewhere where Cecil was listening for it.

The Sea Captain

George reached for the whisky bottle and refilled his glass. It was midday but, still unshaven, still in his scruffy dressng-gown, he was slumped in his sagging armchair, waiting for Harry. His eyes roved over the seedy room with its stained and peeling wallpaper, its unclean, unmade bed, its heavy ugly furniture, his underclothes, trousers, shirt scattered wildly everywhere. It had, he mused, an air of irredeemability befitting its tenant! And the notion made him chuckle — for one thing remaining to George Bennett out of the wreckage of his life was his wry, dry sense of humour.

*　★　*

His landlady came in without knocking — to knock before entering was to show respect.

'That Mr Maxwell's back. Do I show him up?'

'Of course.'

'Doant understand why a gentleman like he is bothers wi' the likes of you.'

'To be quite honest, Mrs Rawlinson, neither do I.'

'An' doant forget it's Friday!' She slammed the door behind her.

George pushed himself to his feet, stood for a moment unsteadily, then, going to the pockmarked mirror, passed a hand across his stubble and, taking a broken comb from his pocket, made a half-hearted attempt at tidying himself. At a knock on the door, he turned, pulling the dressing-gown tighter about himself.

'Come in, Harry!' he called.

Harry came in. About sixty too but upright and well turned out. In his hand were a couple of books.

'Help yourself,' said George, waving vaguely to the whisky bottle.

'I wouldn't want to deprive you,' Harry said resentfully. 'These are all I could find.'

George took the books and glanced at their spines. *Race and colour in Indonesian Literature*, he observed of one.

'Well there's damn all I could find on Sumatra,' Harry said. 'I thought . . . ' But he broke off — his attitude one of defensive hopelessness.

George chuckled. He understood precisely: it was difficult for Harry not to appear either critical or patronising. 'Probably turn out to be just the thing,' he said. He looked at the second book. *From the Cam to the Cays.* 'Couldn't be better. Thanks.'

'You look terrible,' Harry said.

'I know.'

'For God's sake, why not shave? Or, better still, see a doctor.'

'Cheers,' said George, raising his glass.

'If you like, I'll shave you.'

'You're a good chap, Harry.'

'You can't go on like this.'

'No.'

'Then do something.'

'Like what?'

'Pull yourself together. Give up drinking. Get yourself a job.'

George shook a wise head. 'Not much call for commercial travellers of sixty who've taken to the bottle.'

'Couldn't that niece of yours . . . the one you write these ridiculous letters to . . . '

'No. Because of them.'

'It's bound to come out one day. Suppose she turned up here.'

'I know,' said George. He flipped through the pages of one of the books. His eyes brightened. 'How's this, Harry?' he suggested. '*As we left Belize Harbour the city looked a tidy and colourful place, strung out along the shore and melting into mangoes at* its extremities. *But soon this view was left behind and first English Cay and then Rendezvous Cay itself raised a tuft of palms to the skyline.'*

And when Harry did not respond: 'No, Harry, she's not going to turn up here. Because this is the last letter I'm going to write to her. I'll arrange to have it posted from the last port of call. Then I'll die — here in Liverpool.'

'You mean pretend to die?'

'I mean die. Now?' He held up the bottle.

'All right.' Harry sat on the end of the bed.

George handed him his drink. 'You know my trouble, Harry? I've always been a coward. Run away from life. But this . . . ' Again he held up the bottle. 'A friend who doesn't criticize. Like a woman who lets you make love to her without wanting a thousand reasons why. You know, something, Harry? When I started writing to Nicola all those years ago, it wasn't just for her . . . Perhaps it wasn't even for her at all. We all have a bit of Walter Mitty in us, don't we?'

'It *was* for her.'

'Well, maybe. To claim that as the one item on the credit balance sheet isn't really too presumptuous, is it? All the same, I've enjoyed it, Harry. Quite a game it's been: scouring the world for new ports of call. I used to think about it banging my way in mist up the old A.1. I wasn't your average commercial traveller — I was Captain George Bennett on his bridge nosing his way through fog into the St Lawrence Gulf. It suited me . . . because I was a coward. If I hadn't been I'd have taken on responsibility instead of inventing it.'

'You took on responsibility,' Harry said.

'Only by accident. But I did a little good, didn't I, Harry?'

'Yes.'

'Yes. So you see I can't throw the little good I've done away. Crawl into the life of a young girl who doesn't need me any longer. Destroy the image that's kept both of us going. I haven't the guts.'

'You've the guts to kill yourself?'

'What? A couple of bottles and a handful of barbiturates?'

Harry went to the window, untouched drink in hand. He stared over a wasteland to an abandoned factory remembering the George of boyhood. 'When are you going to do it?' he asked quietly.

'Oh, I couldn't say for sure. In about a fortnight's time. I've got to sail back from Belize.'

★   ★   ★

In fact it was nearly a month before Harry met Nicola at the crematorium. She was quite beautiful really, high-cheekboned with big green eyes and a mass of black coarse hair. He could see no family likeness.

'It was kind of you,' she said, 'to write and let me know. He meant a great deal to me.'

'He often spoke of you.'

'He was a wonderful man, wasn't he?'

'Yes. And a better man than he thought himself to be.'

'He used to write letters to me, you know. From all over the world. I've still got them all, you know. Every one. There must be hundreds. He was all I had.'

'And you were all he had.'

'He had you. You're here today. Just you.' And quickly, as if for fear he might speak first: 'He wouldn't have wanted a life which meant a crowd of people like that lot over there.' She nodded towards a group of mourners dutifully reading the cards on a neat oblong of wreaths. 'He couldn't have lived in a suburb. Or a village. He wanted the smell of the sea in his nostrils. He wanted the colour of the tropics not the greyness of an English winter.' And, angrily kicking the pavement: 'He should have died at sea not in a Liverpool lodging house.'

'We live not as we would but as we can.

And die that way too.'

She tossed her magnificent jet black hair. 'He lived as he would. Always. He made life work for him.' And, guiltily: 'When my parents were killed he sort of . . . took over. I used to count the weeks until he came back from a voyage. And he'd come and see me . . . not often, he wasn't in England often enough or long enough . . . And somehow since I've left school it hasn't worked out . . . I should have made a bigger effort.'

'You mustn't blame yourself,' Harry said. 'You never knew when he was coming home. And, my dear child, please believe me when I tell you you gave him as much as he gave you. We all need roots. Even sea captains need roots. And you were his.'

She thought about that. Nodded. 'Yes, you're right. I knew that from his letters. He thought they were only for me but I realised they were for him as well. I think that's why I loved him so much. To love someone you have to be needed. And he needed me. Even up there on his bridge . . . They were big ships, you know . . . At least I always felt they were.'

'Yes, they were big ships. He was highly thought of.'

Harry took out his wallet and withdrew a card. 'If you need help . . . '

'I'll be all right.'

'You'll be all alone now.'

'I'll be all right. You're very kind. And thank you again. Goodbye.'

★ ★ ★

She stood alone, waiting. At length the man came up to her.

'You can have them now if you want,' he said. 'We've got them ready. But are you sure, Miss, you wouldn't rather leave them here? We could let you have an urn. They aren't all that expensive. And we have shelves for them. And you could plant a rose tree with a plaque . . . '

She thought of Singapore. And Barranquilla. Of Takoradi and Aqaba. Of English Cay. 'I don't think he'd have liked a plaque,' she said. 'Would you mind. I've brought a bag.'

'A bag?'

She unzipped her handbag and took out the bag. An ordinary bag of stiff, shiny paper with *Fordyce, Grocers* printed on it. 'I'm sorry,' she said, 'but I only thought about it this morning and there wasn't time . . . '

'Very well,' the man said stiffly. 'Come with me.'

'No. I'll wait here..'

The man took the bag and turned to go; but curiosity overcame him. 'May I ask,' he said, 'how you intend to dispose of them?'

'In the only way I should,' she told him simply. 'He was a very important man, you know. Did you know that?'

He shook his head. 'No.' And, apologetically: 'We have so many, you know. We don't have the time.'

'No, of course you don't. And why should you know, anyway? But he was too big a man to fit into a little urn and be sat upon a shelf.'

★ ★ ★

She caught a bus and then a train and from the station at the other end, she walked down to the beach which wasn't far. She hired a rowing boat and, putting the paper bag next her handbag beside her, paddled a long way out. Then she shipped the oars, undid the bag and gently poured the ashes on the sea which was calm. She watched them and for a moment they seemed to hesitate and then they dispersed and were quite gone. She crunched up the bag and threw it away. And it was very strange for the stiff paper unfolded a little and seemed to reshape itself into something rather like a sailing boat and the breeze drifted it away.

The Gadabout

Andrew Brimble, widower, self-made magnate, left three offspring: Gerald — heavy, dull, insensitive; Winifred — fastidious, active, irritatingly efficient; Bertie — easygoing, frivolous, irrepressible.

After the funeral they repaired to lawyer Caldicot's office for the reading of the will.

'Please be seated,' he directed them, taking his place behind a table, on which rested a single document and an opened Bible, and indicated by a slow wave of a scrubbed white hand three hard wooden chairs which faced him.

They took their seats: on the right Gerald, ponderous, condescending; in the centre, Winifred erect, assertive, censorial; on the left Bertie, slim, lively, hopeful.

'As you will all be provided with a copy of the will,' said Caldicot, 'I propose to dispense with the preliminaries.' His slightly raised eyebrows awaited their consent, then lowered. 'After one or two minor bequests,' he continued, 'we come to the kernel of the matter.' And he read: 'I leave to each of my children the sum of twenty thousand pounds.'

'Only twenty thousand?' said Gerald, fruitily indignant.

'I do not believe it,' said Winifred, very precisely. 'I just do not believe it.'

And Bertie said nothing.

'I have now,' Caldicot continued expressionlessly, 'to read you a passage from the authorized King James' version of the Holy Bible. It is known as the parable of the talents. 'For, (he read), *the kingdom of heaven is as a man travelling into a far country who called his own servants and delivered unto them his goods. And unto one he gave five talents, unto another two and unto another one . . .* ' '

'The point is taken,' interrupted Winifred.

'Do we have to hear it all?' demanded Gerald.

And Bertie remained silent.

'Those are my instructions,' Caldicot answered coldly. And he read on to the end. '' . . . *For unto every one that hath shall be given and he shall have abundance; but from him that hath not shall be taken away even that which he hath.*' ' He closed the Bible.

'And what's that rigmarole all about?' demanded Gerald.

'It's obvious, isn't it?' said Winifred acidly. And to Caldicot: 'How much is there to be shared?'

'After deduction of estate duties and meeting the minor bequests, six hundred and ninety thousand pounds,' the lawyer replied impassively.

Bertie broke his silence with a whistle.

'And what do we have to do?' said Winifred.

'By your own industry turn twenty thousand into one hundred thousand in five years and you will receive two hundred and thirty thousand pounds plus accrued interest; fail and your share goes to certain charitable foundations.'

'Only had to double it in *that*,' grumbled Gerald, jabbing a finger accusingly at the Bible.

'I think,' said Caldicot with the lawyer's crisp contempt for as yet comparatively impecunious legatees, 'your father was aware that with interest rates at current levels all you would have to do to double it would be to deposit it in a bank.' And, without pausing: 'There are two further points. Firstly there is nothing in this will which will provide collateral for anyone to lend you money on; secondly discretion as to whether or not you have met the conditions lies entirely with my firm. I shall look forward to meeting you all again in five years time when you must bring with you such documents as are necessary to satisfy me as to your claims on the balance of the estate.' He rose, but, as they followed suit, showed the first display of interest:

'I am curious to learn in what directions you intend to involve yourselves over the period and so gain your inheritance.' And to Gerald. 'Have you any idea, Mr Brimble, what *you* will do?'

'Certainly,' said Gerald. 'I shall set up in business selling something the public can't do without.'

'Admirable,' said Caldicot. 'And you, Miss Brimble?'

'I,' said Winifred (who like her brother had obviously long known what she wished to do if the opportunity ever arose), 'shall buy a plot of land and go into market gardening. People must eat.'

'Indeed they must,' agreed Caldicot. And to Bertie: 'And finally . . . '

Bertie chuckled. 'I wonder if it's worth it, Mr Caldicot,' he said.

★ ★ ★

All but five years have passed and had the lawyer been able to follow their respective fortunes, he would have observed Gerald (who had chosen sanitaryware as the commodity which the public could not do without) seated at his desk, dictating letters, making telephone calls, designing catalogues and in general working all hours God sent to secure his fortune. And he would have seen Winifred in heavy boots clumping around her smallholding, hoeing, weeding, digging, manuring, lifting, packing, selling and watching her rising bank balance with a cold and calculating eye. Or he would have noted Bertie (seldom alone) enjoying the sunlit days, holidaying abroad, playing the horses, but, judging by the bills arriving and the bank managers telephoning, no nearer inheriting two hundred and thirty thousand pounds plus interest than on the day of his father's funeral.

★ ★ ★

And thus we come to the present and find Bertie in the company of a very pretty girl (whose name is Sally) seated on a rug somewhere in the country. Nearby is his car, a trifle ancient perhaps, but sporty; around them are the remnants of a picnic. It is a glorious day and they are laughing at some shared joke but break off laughing because they are lightly in love and laughter between lovers often leads to kisses. And while she is still in his arms, Bertie whispers: 'Marry me, Sally.'

'No fear,' she says.

'Why not?'

'Because you're a gadabout. You're fun! You laugh! You enjoy life! You make everyone who's with you enjoy life too! But you're a gadabout. And marriage isn't for gadabouts. Marriage is a serious business.' And, more seriously: 'Anyway you couldn't afford to marry me.'

'I nearly could have,' he whispers in her hair.

She pushes him away. 'What was that, you said?'

He looks at her — fresh, young, delicious: 'I nearly could have.'

And he tells her about his father's will.

'How long ago was that?'

'There's one week to go.'

'And how much *do* you have?'

'One hundred and sixty-nine pounds.'

'What did you do with the twenty thousand?'

'Subsidised five bloody marvellous years.'

'H'm,' says Sally. 'I wish I'd known you earlier.'

'Suppose you had? What would you have done? Sat in an emporium helping me sell lavatories or clumped round in wellies planting aubergines? Or shared the moonlight over Capri?'

'I think,' says Sally, 'I'd have settled for the Capri bit. Is that what they do? Gerald? And . . . what's her name?'

'Winifred. She specializes in aubergines.'

'Didn't know aubergines grew in England. Or at least, not commercially.'

'If Winifred says that aubergines are to grow commercially in England, they grow! She's got a new strain and crossed it with cucumbers or something and she's got a greenhouse full of the little darlings all popping through the mulch. It's created quite a furore in the horticultural world. She's bound to end up Dame Winifred of Wroxley.'

'And does she depend on these aubergines . . . '

'To collect her two hundred and thirty thousand? Good Lord no. She'll do that on her head. She's long since got past worrying about such sordid things as money.'

'You mean her life's become her aubergines?'

'I couldn't have put it better.'

'And your brother just sells lavatories?'

'*Just* sells lavatories? You've no idea! When you think of the variety of receptacle that has been invented for human beings to perform a simple, natural function . . . '

'I'll take your word for it.'

'Don't!' Bertie chuckles his engaging chuckle.

'Go and see for yourself. Incredible what he's got. Even one of Queen Victoria's.'

'I don't believe it!'

'His *enfant gaté* Brown had it sent up especially to Balmoral. But it seems Queen Victoria tried it out for size and didn't find it very comfortable so she never used it — and after that Brown wouldn't allow anyone so much as sit on it. And neither will Gerald. He's a terrible snob, you know, and this is the closest he's ever got to royalty. He's plumbed it in and got it on a sort of dais with ropes around it keeping the public off and a dirty great notice screaming its history. Like Winifred's aubergines, it's the big thing in his life. I imagine he bows to it every morning.' He breaks off. 'Sally,' he says severely, 'you are not listening to me.'

She turns her head, leans towards him and lightly kisses him.

'Darling,' she says, 'Do you think either of them would lend you a hundred thousand for a week?'

★ ★ ★

The very next morning they call at Winifred's establishment, by now a many-acred area of greenhouses sheltered behind the high brick walls of what was once the kitchen garden of a mansion and within the entrance a sign:

WINIFRED BRIMBLE.
PURVEYOR OF LUXURY
FRUIT AND VEGETABLES.
TRADE GENERALLY NOT
SUPPLIED.

'Purveyor!' says Sally. 'You have to be Fortnums or better, obviously.'

* * *

From an office close by they are directed towards a distant corner by way of immaculate gravelled paths, and pass between equally immaculate greenhouses in which are men and women in overalls lettered *Brimbles* until finally they arrive at one in which Winifred, identically attired, is working. At their entry, she looks up, alarmed.

'Shut that door!' she cries. 'What are you doing here?'

'I thought you'd like to meet my fiancée,' says Bertie blithely.

'Fiancée!', sniffs Winifred. 'Huh. More fool you. Do you have a job?'

'Not at the moment,' Sally says.

'Then I suggest you start looking for one.'

'What are you doing?' enquires Bertie, hoping to improve the atmosphere.

'Since you ask, dusting my aubergines.'

'Really,' says Sally. 'What for?'

'Against mildew.' And, thawing slightly. 'Don't tell me you're interested in plants.'

'Tremendously,' lies Sally. 'My father grows cucumbers.'

'I hope he dusts them.'

'I really don't know.'

'Tell him he must. Here!' Winifred reaches for an empty packet of dusting powder. 'Tell him to try this kind. Once a week. Without fail. Fool proof. Every previous batch died of mildew until I started using it. But these! Look at them! At last!'

And the triumph possessing her reminds her of a matter which, to tell the truth, is no longer of great importance to her and she rounds on Bertie. 'There's a week to go, isn't there? I suppose you've come to try to borrow money off me.' Bertie nods, reflecting that dissimulation so far as Winifred is concerned will be as ineffective as had apparently been her previous dusting powders.

'Well,' Winifred tells him acidly. 'You're wasting your time.'

Bertie turns to go but Sally stops him, pleading: 'You could manage it couldn't you, Miss Brimble? It would only be for a week.

And we're getting married ... I mean you wouldn't rather it went to a charity than to your brother ...'

'I could manage it on my head,' agrees Winifred, 'but I am not going to. While he' — with a scornful glance at Bertie — 'has been gadding about enjoying himself, his brother and I have been usefully employing ourselves so that now, after our five years, we have something to show for it ...'

'A greenhouse filled with aubergines and a lavatory rejected by Queen Victoria!' chuckles Bertie, seeing it all in a proper perspective. 'What triumphs in return for the sacrifice of five prime years of life!'

★ ★ ★

Nevertheless he is persuaded to try Gerald who they discover seated behind a massive desk in a palatial office. The years have left their imprint and Gerald is now stout, sleek and patronizing. Like his sister he feels called upon to deliver a little homily:

' ... While I must admit I shall find it hard to watch Caldicot handing over to charity what must be not less than three hundred thousand pounds by now, at least I shall be comforted by the knowledge it will not be frittered away on wine, women and song. And in fact with hindsight I have come to the conclusion that father was a far seeing man. He gave us each our opportunity. Winifred and I have taken it and moved on. You, Bertie, have not. That is all there is to it.' And cutting short a not dissimilar riposte to that which Bertie had delivered on Winifred earlier:

'My dear Bertie, the money is no longer of importance. It is succeeding on one's own account which matters. For example, I have this morning coming to see me an American gentleman who is considering placing an order for six hundred lavatories for an hotel which he is building. And do you know how he came to hear of me? Because of the publicity I have obtained worldwide for Queen Victoria's pristine, unused, unsullied lavatory. And he is only the latest of several such interested clients. Glance at it on your way out and reflect on this: that the key to commercial success is to have something to offer which is unique!'

'In your case a lavatory, in your sister's aubergines?' says Sally.

'Precisely,' says Gerald with delight.

★　★　★

It was indeed in its way as impressive an emporium as had been Winifred's market garden boasting a showroom of great length with on both sides an almost endless series of lavatories of every imaginable type and hue and between the lines of them a corridor, floored with soft, deep carpet, which led the eye inevitably to Gerald's masterpiece resting on its carpeted dais, protected from the hoi polloi by burgundy twisted rope with beside it a notice, reading:

THIS CLOSET SET WAS INSTALLED BY JOHN BROWN FOR QUEEN VICTORIA'S USE IN BALMORAL CASTLE. HER MAJESTY FOUND IT NOT ENTIRELY TO HER LIKING. OUT OF HIS GREAT AFFECTION FOR THE QUEEN, JOHN BROWN PLACED AN ABSOLUTE EMBARGO ON ITS USE BY ANY OTHER PERSONS AND IN CONSEQUENCE IT HAS NEVER BEEN USED. GERALD BRIMBLE PURCHASED THIS INTERESTING ITEM TO EXEMPLIFY AND UNDERLINE HIS WISH TO GIVE AN EQUAL SERVICE TO HIS PATRONS AND TO SYMBOLISE THE UNSULLIED QUALITY OF THE GOODS WITH WHICH THE COMPANY WILL ALWAYS DEAL. BY THIS EXAMPLE THE HOUSE OF BRIMBLE STANDS.

'The House of Brimble!' says Sally afterwards. 'Of all the pompous, self-opinionated, idiotic . . . '

'Damn the House of Brimble! And damn the House of Winifred for that matter!' Bertie cries. 'This calls for a celebration!'

'Celebration?' says Sally. 'What? Losing three hundred thousand pounds?'

'No,' chuckles Bertie. 'Not frittering away five whole years of life on aubergines and lavatories. And still having one hundred and sixty-nine pounds to spend! You know what we're going to do? Blow every penny of it on the biggest, slap-up lunch you ever set about. Epicurus will have nothing on us. We're going to the Savoy!'

★ ★ ★

And they do, but, immediately afterwards, trying to stop a cruising taxi, Bertie is run over by a passing car and killed.

★ ★ ★

A day or two later, in Caldicot's office, cheques, each well in excess of three hundred thousand pounds, are handed to Gerald and Winifred. They accept them in the offhand manner of people who have discovered there are more important things than money but as they turn to leave, Caldicot stops them.

'There is one other small matter,' he advises. 'Your brother in his will left all he possessed to you.'

'Pah!' says Gerald.

'Can't be worth a row of beans,' says Winifred.

'Neverthless . . . '

'Give it to that girl,' Gerald suggests. 'Agreed?'

'Agreed,' says Winifred.

'And the ashes? What shall I do with them?' And Caldicot coughs apologetically — for Gerald and Winifred are now to be viewed in a different light. 'He does suggest you might make egg timers out of them.'

Gerald is unmoved and unamused. 'A warped sense of humour,' he observes. 'Want 'em, Winifred?'

'No,' says Winifred. 'Give them to the girl as well.'

★　★　★

A few weeks later Gerald is delighted to be approached by a national newspaper which having apparently heard about Queen Victoria's closet proposes publishing an article upon it. All is arranged and at noon precisely a young man equipped with camera and tape recorder, arrives. After a serving of champagne and caviare, Gerald is interviewed after which the young man advances camera in hand towards the masterpiece. But at this precise moment from amongst the small press of interested spectators a very pretty young woman steps out, ducks neatly under the twisted rope before anyone can prevent her, and taking a paper bag from out of her handbag, empties its contents in the pan and, with gusto, pulls the chain.

'Oh, my God,' shrieks Gerald, too late to intervene, anticipating the catastrophe about to happen, that the rust of a century and more is not to be gainsaid. And sure enough as the water, always religiously topped up, rushes joyously down, the flush pipe begins to bend and the cistern, partly dependant on it, topples and, crashing on to the porcelain pan, smashes it to smithereens.

The camera flashes, all is faithfully recorded for posterity and Sally, for of course the girl is Sally, calls to the photographer: 'Well done, Sam. Time for lunch.'

But Gerald, raising his eyes from the mess of shattered china, twisted metal and rusty water, puts out a hand to stop her leaving.

'What have you done?' he moans.

'Flushed half your brother down the

lavatory,' answers Sally brightly.

He stares at her stunned, releasing her arm, hardly daring to ask the second question.

'And the other half of Bertie?' he manages at length. 'What have you done with that?'

'Oh, that?' says Sally. 'I dropped it in on Winifred.'

He repeats it dully. 'You dropped it in on Winifred.'

'Well,' says Sally. 'Actually I put it in an empty packet of dusting powder and left it in that greenhouse in which she was bringing up her aubergines.' And, after a moment's pause, lightly. 'I hear she's going to try growing capsicums instead.'

★ ★ ★

Over a dry martini, Sam says to her. 'It wasn't Bertie's idea, I take it?'

'No, Sam,' says Sally. But then she pauses. 'Or was it, I wonder. I mean . . . he did choose the Savoy for our final lunch together.'

Sam does not interrupt.

Sally muses a while and then says slowly. 'He told me a little story over that lunch. A true one, you know. About Newton.'

'Gravity and all that?' suggests Sam helpfully.

She shakes her pretty head. 'Not Isaac

Newton. Robert Newton. The actor. You remember him?'

Sam nods. 'Robert Newton. Always played way-out parts. Rum sort of chap he was.'

'Very rum,' says Sally. '*He* left instructions as to the disposal of his ashes you know.'

'Did he really?'

'Yes,' said Sally, still very thoughtful. 'Specific instructions. Seems he had a blistering argument with the Savoy Hotel and to let it be known exactly what he thought of them he left it in his will his ashes were to be flushed down one of their loos. And they were. And, after a pause: 'Funny wasn't it — that Bertie should have told me the story then. Almost as if he knew he'd never get another chance . . . '

The Nagging Tooth

The Rolls Royce bearing the legend SK1 drew up in Berkeley Square and Solly got out and entered his offices through the plate glass door Moss held open.

Moss said. 'Good morning, Mr Kornblath.'

''Morning, Moss.' Solly paused. 'A Miss Bradshaw will be calling. Send her straight up, will you.'

'Yes, Mr Kornblath.' Moss's face was without expression.

Solly crossed the foyer into the lift held open for him, up several floors, along the carpeted corridor to the Boardroom. Coote, Grey, Hamilton and, less quickly, Cradforth, began to rise but Solly waved them down as he sat at the head of the long mahogany table.

'Only one item this morning, Sir,' said Coote, long, thin and nervous, peering myopically at the agenda. 'Burlington House.'

'Where's our architect?'

'He's a little delayed,' Coote apologised.

'Then we'll wait.' He looked at Hamilton who had hard, pale eyes. 'Talking of architects, who d'you think we should have for the Plaxton Centre, Hamilton?'

'I thought . . . Chattock and Finn?'

'Grey?'

Grey was one of the new young men. 'Leon and de Soutar.'

Hamilton pounced gratefully. 'After what they did to Northern Properties at Walsall!'

'Walsall was a tricky situation . . . '

Solly waved for silence. 'Cradforth?'

Hamilton's eyes were hard but Cradforth was hard all through. 'No opinion,' he said crisply.

'Why Chattock and Finn?' Solly asked of Hamilton.

'I can get them at four per cent.'

'You sound,' said Cradforth, 'as if you were buying apples.'

'Could you,' enquired Solly aimiably, 'have got Tod for us on Burlington House at four per cent?'

'I wasn't with you when he was taken on.'

Solly smiled. His face was round, fat, benevolent and he had nice blue eyes. 'Tell you what,' he said, 'we'll settle on Tod for Plaxton too and you see what you can get him for.' For a moment there was no benevolence. 'But see you get him.'

Tod came in just then, short, broad and businesslike. Solly made the introductions: 'Hamilton has taken over as chief surveyor and Grey assists him.'

For an hour they discussed the details of the scheme. Then Solly said: 'Fine. Once we've bought up all the leases, we're in business. How many outstanding, Coote?'

'Three, Sir. Sweet and Matheson; Smith, Lane and Melvin; and a man named Desmond Llewellyn . . . '

* * *

Gillian Bradshaw was young, well turned out, self-assured, undeniably attractive. Moss showed her up by the chairman's private lift. 'Mr Kornblath asked me to tell you to make yourself at home. He's at a Board Meeting but shouldn't be long.'

He left by the lift which opened directly on to the flat and Gillian walked round, inspecting. An opulent sitting-room, a bedroom with double bed, bathroom, kitchen. And everything to hand: cigarettes, magazines — and a bottle of champagne in an ice bucket too near a two seater settee with a small table with two glasses on it too near as well. Gillian smiled and moved the table.

* * *

Coote was coming to an end: ' . . . and then when Mr Melvin . . . '

'Never mind. What does this Llewellyn do?'

'Insurance agent, Mr Kornblath. Just two rooms.'

Solly nodded. 'Right. Until we get those three leases we might as well not have the other thirty-four. I want them all tied up before I go away. Who's handling Sweet and Maxwell?'

Grey explained that Sweet, an engineer, was retiring soon and didn't want the bother of upheaval.

'Mr Tod', Solly said, 'have you ever worked with Sweet?'

Tod smiled the attractive smile which crinkled up his eyes. 'I thought you'd more or less appointed Gunter.'

'Gunter can be disappointed.' Solly picked up the telephone and asked for Sweet. 'What do Smith, Lane and Melvin do?'

'Accountants, Sir,' said Coote.

'Which means they know we want to get on with demolishing and they've done their arithmetic.' Sweet came on the line. 'Ah,' said Solly. 'About your lease, Mr Sweet.' He listened good humouredly. 'Yes, quite, Mr Sweet. But if we can't buy your lease, we can't start demolishing and I'm sure, as an engineer you wouldn't want to see such a prestigious scheme abandoned. And of course there are other forms of compensation. For example we are uncommitted to an engineeer and if you agreed to sell us your lease . . . '

When he was done, Grey, who had been listening spellbound said: 'Are you going to speak to Smith, Lane and Melvin too, Sir?'

'No,' said Solly. 'They're accountants so all they think about is money which makes it just a matter of negotiation. Mr Cradforth will deal with them. So . . . we're left with Mr Llewellyn and his two rooms. What's the problem?'

'He won't answer letters,' said Hamilton, sulking.

'One of yours is he? How many letters has he had?'

'Three. I didn't want to seem too keen. He's in a very small way of business. Doesn't even have a secretary. Anyway he was the least important of the thirty-seven.'

'He's the most important now. What do you think, Tod?'

'That he sounds suspiciously like a nagging tooth.'

'Doesn't he? How much did you offer him, Hamilton?'

'A thousand at first. It's two thousand now.'

'Spoken to him?'

'Twice.'

'And?'

'He was . . . evasive.'

'Yes,' said Solly. 'He would be. The man's obviously heard all about the Solomon Kornblath Investment Trust and knows it's not going to hold up a scheme costing twenty millions for a few thousand pounds. You'd better get on to him again and fix some sort of deal. And, Hamilton — don't let your enthusiasm for buying apples leave you empty-handed.'

★   ★   ★

Gillian, hearing Kornblath coming, lowered her eyes to a magazine. 'Miss Bradshaw?' She looked up — and Solly was delighted with what he saw. 'I'm so sorry', Solly said aimiably. 'I hope you haven't been waiting long.'

'I've been very comfortable, Mr Kornblath.'

'Good.' Solly, noting that the table had been shifted from where he'd placed it personally the previous day, smiled faintly. 'You'll join me in a glass of champagne?'

'That would be lovely.'

'Now,' said Solly as he poured, 'about this post which my good friend, John Campbell, seems to think you could fill admirably. As I expect he's told you, it's my practice to take a winter cruise and I require a private secretary to accompany me. As my wife does not enjoy cruises, my secretary has to . . . ', he paused while he placed the glass of champagne by her, ' . . . has to act as my hostess when the occasion arises and it is essential, as I'm sure you'll appreciate, that she should have certain qualities . . . '

'Quite,' said Gillian. 'Mr Campbell indicated them.'

'Good,' said Solly agreeably. 'I invariably have the same suite which would include what would be your cabin and your stateroom and I do not carry a lot of business with me, so the job will hardly be an arduous one. Does it interest you?'

'It would depend on the salary.'

'The salary is not important.'

'It is to me. I should need a lot of clothes.'

Solly beamed: 'Naturally, Miss Bradshaw, I would be happy to meet any account you ran up equipping yourself.'

'Any account?' She uncrossed her legs and crossed them the other way and smoothed the skirt over her knee. She was wearing a plain black dress and Solly found the contrast of the silken flash delightful.

'Yes. Any account,' he said.

'And would there be a bonus at the end if I proved . . . satisfactory?'

Solly remembered Mr Llewellyn. 'Five thousand pounds,' he said.

'I agree,' said Gillian.

Solly raised his glass: 'To a pleasant voyage, Miss Bradshaw, then,' he said.

*   *   *

The Board Meeting had broken up. 'Must be marvellous,' young Grey was saying, 'to be able to handle people the way Solly handled Sweet.'

Hamilton was sour: 'Anyone can if they happen to be worth what he's worth.'

'Precisely,' Cradforth said. 'How much are you going to offer Llewellyn?'

'I haven't decided.'

'Bet you won't get him for under ten thousand. Nor any change from Tod.' He closed the door behind him.

'Bloody time server,' Hamilton said.

'Aren't we all?' said Coote.

*   *   *

Gillian was on her feet. 'I'm sorry, Mr Kornblath, I already have a lunch appointment.'

'What a pity. I was hoping we might have a little lunch at the Coq d'Or. Tomorrow perhaps?'

'What for?' said Gillian.

'It would be nice to get to know each other better before we leave.'

She looked into his nice blue eyes. He smelt of toilet water and reminded her of a baby — soft, chubby, relaxed, powdered, clean.

'But surely, Mr Kornblath,' she said, 'we understand each other perfectly.'

★ ★ ★

Her arrival in the foyer coincided with Martin Tod's; it was raining heavily but fortunately a taxi was being paid off. 'You take it,' Gillian said. 'I'm sure you're in a hurry.'

'Not in the least.'

'You'll never get another. Not in this lot.'

'Neither will you.'

'All right. Let's share it.'

As they climbed in, Tod said: 'I suppose you aren't free for lunch?'

Gillian looked carefully at him and liked what she saw. 'With one 'phone call I could be,' she said.

'Where would you like to go?'

Gillian chuckled. 'How about the Coq d'Or?' she said.

* ★ *

A man, tall, rather sepulchral looking, came up to their table. 'Why, good afternoon, Miss Bradshaw,' he said with some surprise.

Gillian looked up. 'Oh, good afternoon, Mr Campbell. Fancy seeing you here.' She made the introductions.

'I had rather expected to see Mr Kornblath here as well,' Campbell said.

'He's changed his plans,' said Gillian brightly.

'Nothing wrong I hope? Good. Well my apologies for disturbing you.'

'An undertaker?' Tod enquired, watching Campbell depart.

She laughed. 'In a way.' She sipped her coffee. 'What exactly are you doing for Mr Kornblath, Martin?'

'Handling a twenty million pound office block.'

'Tell me about it.'

'It's held up by a nagging tooth.' And, at her frown. 'By a man named Desmond Llewellyn who, if he doesn't sell his lease, is quite going to spoil Solly's holiday. He's due off on a Caribbean cruise.'

'Really? And do you think his holiday will be spoiled?'

'I doubt it. He has the power to be

99

persuasive. May I ask what you were doing with Mr Kornblath?'

She smiled. 'Just discussing a matter of business.'

'Just business?'

'Yes.'

'Then can we meet again?'

She hesitated, then agreed. 'It can't be for a little while.'

'The first free day you have.'

Gillian consulted her diary: 'Friday, twenty-eighth of February,' she said.

★　★　★

Hamilton was making a telephone call: 'He's not back from lunch! But, dammit, it's after three! Well please tell, Mr Grey, when he deigns to come back from lunch, to make sure that Brighton bid goes off. If there's anything on it he doesn't understand he can get me at Mr Llewellyn's. Have you got that Miss Petersen. At Mr Llewellyn's . . . Yes. I am. Face to face!'

He stepped out from the box and, with the air of a man who has stood quite enough nonsense for one day and is going to have no more of it, set off to deal with the irritating Mr Llewellyn and was so enwrapped by this mood that he quite ignored another man who passed him on the steps. The building he entered was quite dramatically empty with doors on each floor open, papers discarded everywhere, abandoned furniture and the lift no longer operating. This evidence of past success merely hardened the glint in Hamilton's cold eyes as he mounted, floor by floor, to the very attic top. But here a closed door faced him and pinned to it a still wet scrawl: *Gone on holiday. Back Friday week.* Hamilton stared at the note horror-stricken, dared to touch it with his fingertip and then was wheeling round, racing down the stairs, leaping whole flights ... But this totally uncharacteristic energy was wasted for the London streets had quite swallowed Desmond Llewellyn up.

★　★　★

On the day Llewellyn was due to return there was another Board Meeting of the Solomon Kornblath Investment Trust.

'... the contracts with Sweet and Matheson have been exchanged, Mr Kornblath,' Coote was saying. 'Smith, Lane and Melvin are exchanging this afternoon.'

'What did they cost us?', Solly asked.

'Fifty-four thousand pounds.'

'It's a lot of money.'

'They had a lot of space,' Cradforth said.

'Yes,' Solly agreed. 'It's reasonable. So . . .'
He eyed a troubled Hamilton. 'We're just left
with Mr Llewellyn.'

There was a silence as if Hamilton was
waiting for a gun to start him off — and then
it was a gabble. 'I haven't been able to
contact him, Mr Kornblath. He's . . . he's
vanished. Into thin air.' Then eagerly: 'But
he's due back at twelve today. I'm having him
tried every ten minutes. And I've told Miss
Petersen to put him through the *moment* she
gets him.'

'Admirable,' said Solly dryly. 'But hasn't it
occurred to you, Hamilton, that it is rather
suspicious that our Mr Llewellyn who is in
such a small way of business and doesn't even
have a secretary should take a holiday at this
time of year?' Hamilton nodded unwillingly
and Solly nodded back at him, a tube of pink
flesh rolling over his collar. 'If ever,' he said, 'I
saw a nagging tooth, it is our Mr Desmond
Llewellyn and I only hope for your sake the
weather we are having here doesn't tempt
him . . .'

The telephone rang just then. Solly put out
a fat hand then paused, and smiling, waved
the call to Hamilton: 'Yours, I imagine,' he
said genially.

It was a long way to walk and so silent was

102

the room that the shush of Hamilton's shoes on the carpet was clearly audible.

'Yes?' His voice was strained, but eager. 'Yes. Put him through. What! But I have to speak to him. It's . . . vital!' He said no more, just listened, then rattled the receiver down. He dared look at no one. 'He's . . . he's in Marrakesh. He's cabled to say . . . that with the weather we've got here . . . ' He trailed off.

'Is that all?' snapped Solly whose eyes were less nice than usual.

'No.'

Solly spoke very slowly. 'Who *was* that Hamilton? Who were you speaking to?'

'Someone from . . . ', he scarcely dared voice it, 'from . . . Kramer's office.'

'Kramer!' It was the first time Grey had heard Kornblath shout.

'Who . . . ?' he began, then thought better of it.

'And I believe,' said Solly, quiet again, but very dangerous, 'you told us, Mr Hamilton, that you offered Mr Llewellyn two thousand pounds for his miserable two rooms.' He shook his head quite slowly. 'I doubt if it will be quite enough, you know.' He addressed the meeting generally. 'Our Mr Llewellyn seems to have worked it out. Our Mr Llewellyn obviously knows all about nagging teeth. *And*

103

all about the Solomon Kornblath Investment Trust. He knows we're not going to abandon a twenty million pound scheme for a paltry few thousands. So what does he do?' He seemed to be enjoying it, pleased there was a Mr Llewellyn. 'Acts the innocent. Lets us buy up all the other leases and get totally involved then hands it over to the professionals.' And to Hamilton alone: 'And chooses the toughest professional in the business!' He picked up the telephone. 'Get me Mr William Kramer.' And putting the receiver down: 'How much, Mr Hamilton, d'you think we're going to have to pay for Mr Llewellyn's two small rooms?'

Out of the morass, Hamilton remembered Cradforth's bet. 'Ten thousand pounds,' he whispered.

'Ten thousand pounds.' Solly could not have been more pleasant. 'You know what you are, Hamilton? A bloody fool.' The telephone rang. 'Kramer?' said Solly. 'Kramer, I have here a man who tells me your Mr Llewellyn is going to want ten thousand for his lease. What do I tell him?' As he listened, a grim smile crossed his face. 'You'd better come round, Kramer . . . No. Today . . . Because, as you know perfectly well, I'm off to the Caribbean before your man comes back!'

'You seem, Mr Hamilton,' he observed over

the returned receiver, 'to be a trifle low. The figure is two hundred and twenty thousand.' He crossed to the door, then paused.

'Oh, Hamilton,' he said goodnaturedly.

'Yes, Mr Kornblath.' The words were barely audible.

'Use the three weeks while I'm away, will you, trying to think of one good reason why I should keep you?'

★   ★   ★

There were flowers everywhere and champagne.

'To a very enjoyable trip, Miss Bradshaw', Solly said handing her a glass.

'Why, thank you, Mr Kornblath,' said Gillian. She sipped a little wine before putting it down and taking off her coat.

'But, surely,' Solly said, 'that's the dress you came to see me in?'

'Yes, Mr Kornblath.'

'But all those new clothes?'

'Oh, I shall wear them. When it's appropriate.'

He patted her hand. 'It's appropriate now.' He chuckled. 'Gillian, isn't it? Or do you prefer Gilly?'

'I prefer, Miss Bradshaw.'

'Oh, but I can't call you Miss Bradshaw for

three weeks,' chided Solly, amused.

'I don't see why not?' She looked around. 'Where do you think I should have my office?'

Solly chortled: 'Where do you think?'

'Perhaps over there?' She was very serious. 'Of course I shall need a table. I imagine you've arranged a Fax and Word Processor. I did bring my portable but . . . '

'I think,' said Solly, still chuckling but a trifle less confidently, 'your portable will do.'

'Oh, but you don't get anything like the same quality . . . '

'It doesn't matter.'

'Oh, but it does!' Her voice was eager. 'I mean to earn every penny of that bonus to say nothing of the salary and all those beautiful clothes . . . '

'Those beautiful clothes were not bought for typing in.'

'No. You explained I might sometimes have to act as hostess . . . '

'And . . . ' there was a touch of grimness now, 'that you were expected to have other qualities. Of course if there has been any misunderstanding . . . '

He broke off as a hooter sounded.

'Oh, I do hope not,' Gillian said anxiously. 'Because if there has been it's too late now to do anything about it.'

'Gillian!' said Solly with a tremendous effort.

'No, Mr Kornblath, Miss Bradshaw, please. I'm sure we'll get on so much better.' Solly slowly, and not without admiration, shook his head. 'And I promise you,' Gillian went on brightly, 'I'll be the best secretary you ever took on any of your cruises. I daresay there were some you regretted afterwards?' Solly nodded — reluctantly. 'Well you won't regret me, Mr Kornblath, I promise.'

★　★　★

Three weeks and a day later Solly's chauffeur met them at Southampton. They were both bronzed and fit and Solly's eyes bluer than ever. He had been the envy of his contemporaries. Never had a man as mature been so mollycoddled by a girl so pretty. Never had his library books been exchanged so thoughtfully, his diet been more scrupulously watched, his drinks so perfectly iced, his rug so carefully tucked around him.

They drove to London and, on a thought, Solly leaned forward and said to his chauffeur. 'Might as well go by Burlington House, Matthews, and see how they're getting on'. He turned to look regretfully at Gillian. 'I like that,' he said.

'What, Mr Kornblath?'

'The suit.' He said it almost with a sigh. For Gillian looked more than lovely — she looked tantalisingly desirable and quite beyond his reach. 'You never wore that on the ship,' he added with faint reproof.

'There never was the occasion,' Gillian said.

*　*　*

When they reached the site, Solly said: 'Like to see how they're getting on?'

She shook her head, a neat head framed in the deep fur collar of the suit. 'No, I don't think so.' And, gathering her handbag. 'I'll pick up a taxi here.'

'Matthews can drive you anywhere.'

'No. I'll get a taxi.'

He was hurt: 'As you choose.'

She wrinkled her nose. 'It's better really.' She held out her hand. 'Thank you, Mr Kornblath. It's been a marvellous experience.'

'I'm glad you enjoyed it so much.'

She smiled at the dryness. 'Oh, but I did.' She hesitated. And then, speaking with genuine regret: 'I'm sorry if I didn't turn out to be quite the secretary you thought I might have been.'

'Perhaps if you'd known me better at the start . . . '

'Perhaps.'

He paused, then chuckled: 'But to be honest . . . '

'On the whole you're rather glad I wasn't.'

He nodded. 'Here!' he said.

'What's that?'

'Your bonus.'

Gillian looked for quite a little time at the cheque for five thousand pounds, then handed it back. 'No', she said. 'I didn't earn it.'

'Just a minute.' She had been about to leave him. 'You could simply have not turned up at Southampton,' he said. 'You'd been paid in advance. You had your clothes.'

'What would you have done then?'

'Cancelled the trip most likely. Come back to London.' He smiled ruefully. 'If you hadn't turned up it would have saved me best part of a quarter of a million pounds that was extorted out of me before I could get this thing going.'

'Really!' said Gillian. 'Oh, dear. Well never mind.' And on a sudden impulse she put her hand on his arm and leaning across, lightly kissed him. And then she was gone. Solly sighed. But he was a resilient man. There were other things in life.

Under the usual sign *The Solomon Kornblath Investment Trust* were the names of those employed: builder, architect, engineer, quantity surveyor. There was the observation platform which made for such good public relations. Solly mounted it and stared into the vast pit of wet and soggy clay through which bulldozers were crawling. Three weeks ago a building had stood here, three weeks ago a man named Desmond Llewellyn . . .

'Mr Kornblath!'

Solly's eyes shifted to the man shouting up to him. 'Tod!', he called.

'Have a good trip?'

'No complaints,' called Solly.

'You certainly look well.'

'I was well looked after. How's it going?'

'Fine.'

'Good.' He paused, feeling lonely. 'Doing anything for lunch?' he called down.

'Sorry. Got a lunch engagement.'

'Another time,' called Solly. A young man had mounted the platform and was standing beside him. 'Looks like a big job, doesn't it?' said Solly, feeling an urge for human companionship. The young man nodded. 'Surprising', Solly went on, 'what a difference

110

it makes. Remember what it was like before they pulled the old one down?'

'Yes', said the man. 'Matter of fact I do.' He stabbed the air with his pipe. 'Matter of fact I had an office up there once.'

Solly was all attention. 'When was that?'

''bout a month back. Matter of fact the people putting this lot up bought my lease. Still haven't got used to it.'

'Used to what?'

'Being rich. Know what they paid me? Two hundred and twenty thousand pounds. And for what? Two poky little rooms with four years left to run. Amazing.'

'Remarkable', said Solly. 'They must be very substantial people.'

'So I'm told.'

'Told? But . . . you must have known. To have put it over on them for so much . . . '

But the man was shaking his head.

'Never *heard* of them. That's the only reason I got two hundred and twenty thousand.' He became communicative. 'You see when they first wrote, offering me a thousand, I threw their letter into the wastepaper basket.' He chuckled. 'Thought it was another damn catchpenny circular. Never heard of them you see. If I had, I'd have taken it like a shot. I was going to move anyway. It wasn't all that convenient.'

'So what happened?' Solly asked very quietly.

'Well they kept pestering me and I happened to mention it to a chum of mine and he suggested I'd better see this man called Kramer.'

'Kramer', Solly echoed.

The man nodded. 'That's right. Professional negotiator. He handled it from then. I just did what he told me.'

'And that was all?'

'No,' said the young man, now cheerfully puffing at his pipe. 'There was something else. But not quite the sort of thing you'd tell a stranger. Well . . . must be off . . . appointment . . . '

★   ★   ★

Solly went back to his car, feeling stunned and lonelier than ever.

'Office, Sir?', said Matthews.

The idea was repugnant. 'No,' said Solly. 'The Coq d'Or.'

★   ★   ★

He was finishing his second martini and contemplating a third when Tod came in, looking around for Gillian. 'Tod!' he called.

'Good Lord,' said Tod. 'Now there's a coincidence.'

'Don't often see you here.'

'No. Keep it for special occasions.'

'Of course,' said Solly, twigging, 'you're meeting someone, aren't you?'

'And here she is,' said Tod. But then he frowned — for Gillian wasn't by herself. There was a young man with her, a young man who only a little earlier had stood beside Solly on his observation platform. Both of them stared at Gillian as she advanced towards them, the young man by her side. She looked quite bewitching with sparkling eyes and her face framed in expensive fur.

'Mr Kornblath,' she cried. 'Oh what an odd coincidence! And Mr Tod! Gentlemen, allow me to introduce — Mr Desmond Llewellyn, my fiancé.'

The River

On the dead grey tree the rooks are
  silhouettes against a pallid sky
The starlings squabble endlessly
  . . . then rest
Sharpening their beaks upon the wires
  which run from pole to pole
And fan their wings in morning
  cleanliness.
The mill is shadowless
White weatherboards — painted long
  ago
And grey-black casements staring
  sightlessly
At a placid stream which once was
  turbulent.
There is a tower that grows from out
  the purple-slated roof
Which bears a simple weathercock
  wrought by a long dead smith
And tells a tale of western wind
That died the night before.
The river now is still enough for the
  barest touch of a fish's mouth
  sucking a fly to stir a trembling
  circle

But for the weir which sings a fruity,
  chuckling song
And spills its silken skirt over the weed-
  softened cill into the pool below.
Green rushes push impatiently between
  the faded broken fronds
And point the death of winter.
The grass is soft, and gay with celandine
  beside the river bank,
From the stony field, ploughed red,
  pheasants, red as the earth itself hurl
  from the morning mist
And in the meadow sudden hares are
  statues for an instant.
The sun is yellow through the haze
But where it picks the prickled stream it
  turns to floating gold.
A shot from somewhere thuds across
  the sky and dies behind the woods,
An April cuckoo calls
The sound of pigeons from the wood is
  soft
And high above the swans whine
  through the dawn.
Who can describe a swan, gliding in
  silence on a river
With feathers trimmed to catch the
  barest breeze
And neck as long as dignity and grace
  can be

And whitemess pure as innocence?

There is so little which man fashions
    which adds a jot or tittle to the scene
A gate perhaps, a fence . . .
But that is nature taking back its own
And moulding it once more to beauty,
Peeling away the harsh and formless
    paint,
Bleaching the wood by sun and wind
    and rain and frost and time,
Bowing the post and rails from their
    mathematical exactitude
To a crookedness
Which blends at last into the
    countryside.

What is that man leaves beside a river
    bank?
A rubber shoe,
A dirty bottle with a plastic cap,
A battered can, the rust not quick
    enough
To blur it to invisibility against the
    background of last season's fallen
    twigs
Which soon, at least, will rot,
A twisted, rusted hawser,
An evil smear of oil,
A rotting tyre, bloated and despondent.

But nature leaves a knot of hair, red
    brown and soft upon a thorn,
A quill, an empty nest,
Discarded blossoms floating on the
    stream,
And Winter's remnants which the
    Spring will hide.

But here the river twists and offers up a
    town, a church, tiled roofs and
    crooked cottages!
These are the things of yesterday,
The time that came and went before
    man's brilliance
Raped serenity
And chased it to such places as he
    could not reach.

We live not as we would but as we can,
    you say . . .
And so it is.

Then choose a house beside a tumbling
    weir
Whose noise will drown the harsh,
    crude, gritty sound of men and yet
    permit
The song of birds in willow trees beside
    the river
To reach your ear.

Where you can see a moorhen build its
  nest
And watch the timid heron
Loping its pterodactyl flight across an
  empty sky
And think, at least, how the river's tale
  is endless
And was there before there was a man
  to hear it
And will be, when the last has gone.

Cairan

As I closed the door of my house in Chester Square, certain I would never sleep in it again, I knew that sense of freedom which comes to schoolboys as they leave school on the last day of summer term — that conscious awareness of the world outside and all it has to offer.

Deciding against the motorway, I chose a route to Settle which would take much longer — for what was the point of hurrying merely to have hours of impatient waiting at the end? And because I had the whole of a long and perfect summer day, I found the drive untiring. I remember that road as a friendly thing — I liked the sound of it beneath my wheels and the echo, echo, echo of spaced posts at corners. I liked the lazy coils of smoke, the sparrows to be slowed for, the tiny incidents and bits of humour. I liked the hot sun beating down, the cool of beer in a village pub, the pressure of wind against my arm, the comicality of a signpost with half its message carried off by a passing lorry. I liked the sheer length of that endless day and I liked it quietly — it was only as it began to lose its fire, as the names of towns — Ilkley, Skipton, Hellifield — spoke meaningly and the traffic flow began to thin, that I began to feel the movements in my belly and the catches at my heart.

★   ★   ★

Cairan, who was leaving Timmy to stay with her aunt, and spending the night at Pen y Ghent 'for the fun of it', had doubted if she'd get there until about eleven. It was a long yet curiously satisfying evening. I ate as late as was permitted, went up to my room to freshen up for her and came down from it at about half past ten with the idea of having a brandy in the bar. As I reached the landing overlooking the foyer, the front door opened and Cairan came in. She looked straight up at me as if she sensed I would be standing there and the next moment she was flying up the stairs and in my arms. Her voice was breathless, saying just the one thing before we kissed: 'I'm shaking all over, Mark!'

★   ★   ★

We went to the bar and talked trifles. Of our journeys up and that this bar, so warm and busy, had been of all things her old headmistress's study. The greatest joy of that pleasant half hour before we went up to her room was that we knew no sense of furtiveness. We were a man and a woman openly in love. When we left it was with our arms about each other.

★ ★ ★

I went in first. She followed me, shut the door and said with simple finality: 'I'm glad that you were there.'

'On the landing?'

'Yes.'

'I was on the way down. And then the front door opened. And you were there. And you looked up at me. As if you knew I was there as well.'

'I did.'

I put my arms around her and held her against me and we didn't kiss because the closeness was enough. Then I put her a little away from me to look at her. She was wearing mauve slacks and a tunic in a pattern of the same sort of colours which came to just below her slender hips and was gathered in a metal link belt around her waist. It was dressy for someone staying alone in an hotel which had once been her school just for the fun of it.

121

'How on earth did you get away with that?' I said.

'I said I had to mend it.'

'What's the matter with it?'

'Nothing. Where's your room?'

'Along the passage.' I remembered something. 'Yours was locked. You said you'd leave it open.'

'You didn't phone me yesterday, so I couldn't tell you where it was. How did you know?'

'I looked in the hotel register. I did phone. But it was a bit late. Timmy answered it.'

She frowned. 'He didn't tell me.' As if it were wrong a little boy hadn't told his mother her lover had phoned.

'I tried again.' I said. 'In the afternoon. About half past four.'

'So that was you. I wondered if it might have been. I was in the bath.'

'I might,' I teased her, 'have been phoning to say I couldn't make it.'

She shook her head. Her thick mass of hair swung, and settled. 'No,' she said.

'I left a note in mine,' I said, 'In case you were early.'

'You are thorough, aren't you? What did you do? Go for a walk?'

'Yes. Down to the river. It was a little misty

but very beautiful. I was thinking of you all the time.'

'I should hope you were.'

'I haven't thought of anything else all day. And yet I wasn't really thinking of you. Just of . . . being. And us. You know what I mean?' She nodded. 'I thought eleven would never come and yet in a way I didn't want it to.'

'I know.'

'And then you were early.'

'I couldn't wait.'

She left me and went across to the basin in the corner by the window and I saw her look at me in its mirror. Her fingers were on a button of her tunic.

'Let me undress you,' I said.

She dropped her hand and waited, looking at me all the time. In the end I did no more than undo the tunic buttons and half pull it off her shoulders to kiss the skin. I felt her shiver and then she had slipped past me and was undressing quickly, putting her things on a chair until she was naked but for her bra.

'Finish me off,' she said and I undid the bra catch and let it fall to the floor and felt her smooth cool skin as far as my hand could reach. She shuddered and pressed against me.

'There's no hurry,' I said. 'For once there isn't any hurry.'

'No.'

She broke away from me and lay down on the bed. 'Hurry all the same,' she said.

I undressed and lay beside her. It was the first time we had ever shared a bed.

'I can't feel,' I said, holding her, 'the shaking.'

'It's inside me. Oh, Mark. Dearest.'

'There's a million things I should be saying to you,' I said.

'It isn't you. It's everything else. Timmy. Philip. Even Aunty Dinah. If there were just us . . .'

'Cairan,' I said. But she stopped me.

'Not yet, Mark. I'm not ready yet.' She sighed. 'Philip will be so hurt.'

'What will he do?'

She thought about it for some time, which was rare for Cairan. She was usually quicksilver in decision.

'I don't really know,' she said. 'But he'll be hurt. Terribly. Having his trust killed.'

'Do you mind that much? Inside yourself?'

'No,' she said. 'It isn't his business. It isn't anyone's business, is it, Mark?'

'No.'

She sat up suddenly

'What is it?' I asked.

'I didn't bring your things.'

'Things?'

'Shaving things. I want to watch you shaving in the morning.'

'I'll fetch them later.'

'Now.'

'I want to make love to you.'

She chuckled. 'We've got all night. And first I'm going to get your things. Where's your key?'

'Trouser pocket.'

She slipped off the bed and I watched her go naked to the door where her dressing gown was hanging. She was wonderfully formed but very small — it always surprised me. But wheh she put on her dressing-gown, which was made of heavy stuff, she was instantly taller.

She found the key, looked at it. 'Forty-seven,' she said, holding it aloft like a prize and was gone.

I got off the bed and, turning the main light off, went to the window and stared at the misty night. 'Philip'll be so hurt,' she'd said. 'Will be.' I felt a wonderful sense of ownership. It was as if all my life till now I'd owned nothing and now I owned the world. I turned at the click of the door and she was back carrying my towel, my dressing gown and shaving things. I watched her putting them, womanlike, in their proper place above the basin. And then she said, stealing my words: 'I don't know when I was so happy.'

*   *   *

We made love, greedily. It had never been like this before between Cairan and myself. All the sensual subtleties available to a man and woman were there for us with a whole night ahead and a bed to share. It was more than passion and more than sex; it was a desire from both of us to prove our love.

*   *   *

Cairan left me and went to the window. The mist had thinned and there was starlight which edged her silhouette with a line of silver. It was an uncanny, almost holy sight, that line of silver edging her throat, breast and belly until the cill cut off the light.

'What can you see?' I asked her softly.

'Just the nearer trees. It's still misty. But you can see the stars.' It was so quiet that when she stopped speaking I could hear the movement of her hair. 'I'm going to open the window,' she told me. 'Come and keep my back warm.'

She said it in the childish way which was half fun and half provocation that she sometimes used when speaking to me. It was one of the things which made her so dear. One of so many things: her quickness and her certainty; her gaiety and openness. And above all this sense of permanent youth.

I went up behind her.

'I often used to stand here looking out,' she told me. 'I used to sleep here you know. That was why I chose this room. There were three of us. And two prefects slept next door. We had to be very quiet. The walls are thin.'

'It's extraordinary,' I said, 'to think of you being at school here. If you could have imagined that one day you'd come back and be made love to in the same bedroom . . . '

I felt her hair brush my face. 'I never thought of things like that.'

'Never thought of being made love to?'

'Never.' She sighed. 'We've got so much to learn about each other, haven't we?'

'That's not a sighing matter.'

'No, it isn't, is it?'

'You'd better come back to bed,' I said. 'You're getting cold.'

★　★　★

'Is this making a difference between you and Philip, sexually?' I asked.

'I don't like him kissing me.'

'But you don't mind him making love to you?'

'No, that's all right. I pretend it's you. But I can't bear him kissing me!' She wriggled in my arms.

'Hasn't he noticed anything?'

'I don't think so.'

'But he loves you?'

'Yes.'

'Did you ever love him?'

'I couldn't have, could I? When I've never loved anyone but you.'

'Why did you marry him?'

'Because you'd gone off and left me on the shelf. He took me down.'

'Tell me,' I said, 'about your being here. Were you happy?'

'Yes. Yes, I was.'

'And this room? Were you in it for long?'

'Three or four terms.'

'Where was your bed?'

'In the corner. Where the dressing table is.'

She told me about her schooldays; who she had shared the bedroom with and what they had been like. Whenever she looked as if she was coming to an end, I prompted her. She was quite right — there was so much we had to learn about each other.

I listened in silence and suddenly she said: 'I know what you're doing.'

'What?'

'It isn't a bedroom to you. It's a dormitory. Where's your dirty mackintosh?'

In a way she was right. I had been imagining her. The same body only younger; the same inner being; the legs and hands and face and hair changing all the time to the legs entwined with my own, the hands keeping me gently ready for sex, the face warm and soft against my neck, the hair brushing my skin like a caress with every breath she took.

'You ought,' she chided me, 'to be ashamed of yourself. A girl of my age too.'

'It's an offence,' I said.

'Don't you care?'

'No.'

'Neither do I. Shall I do that one day?'

'What?'

'Dress up like a schoolgirl for you?'

'Black woollen stockings?'

'Gym slip. White blouse. Everything.'

'And your hair in a pigtail?'

'With a bow in it. Shall I?'

'Would you like to?'

'Well it might be fun. You can pretend to rape me.'

'I don't want to rape you.'

'Oh.' She pretended disappointment. Then her mood changed suddenly.

'I wonder,' she said, 'what Philip would do if he knew I was here with you.' And, after a moment: 'I haven't thought about that very much. Except that's it awful in a way, isn't it, Mark, that one can be so good about it.'

'And so many things to think about.'

'Little things,' she agreed. 'Like car park tickets. Of course, you're very thorough. Throw them away at once. It's disgraceful the way you litter the countryside. You know what I had with Timmy, time before last?' *You don't buy Smarties, Mummy. You don't like them.* And I don't. Only you didn't know. And there they were. In the pigeonhole.'

'So what did you say?'

I knew what Timmy looked like. I'd followed Cairan back once and waited just along the kerb from his school while she collected him. And as they'd passed, I'd seen him look at my car and say something to her and she had smiled at me.

'Oh,' she shrugged. 'I told him I just saw them. He soon forgot. They do, don't they? They've so many more important things to think about. But today I could have murdered him.'

'Why?'

'He talked all the way up. And all I wanted to do was think of you. I should have felt guilty, shouldn't I? With Timmy beside me.

But all I could do was think of you and shake all over.'

She sat up suddenly. 'I've got something for you.'

Abruptly she switched on the light and went, slight and naked, to the dressing table. She opened her handbag, which was lying on it, and took out a letter.

'There,' she said.

Her handwriting hadn't changed. It was firm, sure, flowing, upright, bold and every letter clear. I was back all those years to the store of love letters I had, in one splendid moment, destroyed.

She sat on the bed, her knees hugged tight against her breasts, her hair thrown forward like a screen, watching me.

'*Today, Mark,*' I read, '*I thought of you all day with sheer, effortless indulgence. I was able to trap myself in an invisible mist which no one could penetrate. Breakfast and to school, just a dream. All in a dream the day swept by so quickly . . . lunch, three or four children to tea became just a slight noise in the background. Dinner at night and some friends of Philip's arrived later on in the evening whom, of course, I'd forgotten all about. All managed with a minimum of concentration, my thoughts of us quite uninterrupted. A sort of fantasy not to be*' indulged in too often, it's almost like being two people at once, a private world one can slip into with surprising ease.'

I looked at her and her eyes were on me. I read on. '*I cannot see how this can end, feeling about you as I do now. I think we had the end a long time ago and this, for me, is just a beginning. I can survive without feeling too desperate from week to week but how long before I need you more? It really doesn't bear thinking about . . . far better to exist as we are and not look too far ahead. How little they know . . . but then I'm confused now, I need you all the time, wanting to love, to make love, is dependant on so many different things . . .*

That was all. No signature, no ending. She put out her hand. 'Tear it up?' I shook my head. 'I'll put it in your pocket, then.'

I watched her putting the letter into my coat pocket and felt strangely sad for the slightness of her, for a waist so small for a woman who had borne a son. There seemed so little of her.

When she came back to me, I said: 'Cairan, we've . . . '

She allowed me to go no further. 'Please, Mark, not yet . . . And not now.'

'I've been dead,' I told her. 'All these years. I died the day I left you and now you've brought me back to life.'

'Shh!' And, when I was silent, she said with sadness: 'Perhaps you'd get tired of me if you could see me all the time. Get me out of your system.'

'I never could do that.'

For a moment she didn't speak and then she said, in a puzzled way: 'You know, I couldn't have loved Philip at all, could I? I knew I didn't at the beginning and then I thought I'd learnt how to. And then I met you again. And it was gone. Just gone.' I felt her body tense. 'Listen!'

'What?'

'Listen!'

I listened. The hotel was quiet now. There was just the silence of the night, the creak of boards, the whisper of our bodies against the sheets. Then I heard the owl, hooting somewhere in the mist.

'An owl,' I said.

'Shh!' We listened together, hard against each other and heard the owl again.

'It's magic,' I whispered. 'Lying here with you against me and that owl out there in the swirling mist . . .'

'Shh!' she said again. 'Don't talk. Listen.'

We lay still until we heard the owl again and suddenly her hand was on me: 'Mark!'

'Yes, Cairan?'

'Make love to me again ... Sort of ... quietly, will you? You know, quietly. And then when either of us hears an owl, we'll think of each other ... whatever's happened ... '

Rosie

Not me, it's the people that say,
That the men are leading the women astray,
But I say, that the women of today,
Smarter than man in every way.

Antigua Brute Force Steelband calypso

The only relationship Rosie had ever had with white men was through sex and it was through sex she judged them — usually poorly. In her experience they either wanted it donkey way, or some other dirty way, or could barely hold out between door and bed. And then, when it was over, as often as not they delivered a lecture or enquired of her how she'd got herself involved in such a life — which was a ludicrous question when what they really should have been asking was why other girls who could have done the same spent their lives trudging along the dusty roads into St John's with basket loads of vegetables on their heads.

To Rosie sex was as much the background to her life as Antigua's skies, hills, sun and sea. As had her brothers and sisters all crowded into one small room, she had witnessed it between her father and mother from infancy before experimenting with her brothers early, with the sons of neighbours later and losing, without any sense of loss, her virginity at twelve to a young man who coached her in the miracle of the pill. And so she had no hang ups — sex was something you did either to please yourself or others and sometimes, as with Sanders, both.

Sitting on a bar stool in St John's 'Shady Side Club' she felt definitely superior. Den-nis had said nice things to her last night: told her that she had tits like pears and a bum as smooth and firm as a couple of nice crisp apples and wasn't a bad little fuck at all. He had been rough-faced but gentle-handed, steeped in rum but not ill-humoured and as strong and lasting as any nayga. And tonight he had given Mistress Nerissa all those dollars and was paying for everything which obviously included her, so why shouldn't she sit on the stool whatever Beryl thought and anyway it wasn't Beryl's business but Mistress Nerissa's.

So she sat diminutive but decorative in her white shirt tied into a knot at her navel and scarlet pedal pushers, under the shadow of and, as she felt, sheltered by Den-nis's unchallenged presence.

★ ★ ★

They were talking about last night's cane fire up at Pinkney's Pimple with Sylvester, who always talked a lot, holding forth over the general buzz:

'Me brudder, Willard, done speak wit' Clarence Rowe an' him say he recken it mos' probably Milwood James what lit it. Him got the sack las'week. Him hard-ears and him not forgive that easy.'

'Tchut, you talking foolish,' Tacky, as loquacious as Sylvester, said. 'How many times Millwood James done got sacked this year?' He held up a calloused hand and splayed out the fingers. 'Four times. Him always getting sacked. It him way of life. So why should he risk getting ketched and put in prison. I recken it more like Rassymus. Him in here las' week grumbling 'bout that cane. It very sharp that kind of trash.' He turned to Nelson. 'You saw his hand. All cut up.'

'Like he been through fairy bamboo grove.' Nelson agreed. 'An' burnt cane easier to cut.'

'Erasmus too pyaa pyaa,' Sylvester scoffed. 'Him skeered of him own shadow. It Willwood James for sure. Don't you think that right, Mister Sanders?'

'No,' said Sanders. 'And you can get in trouble Sylvester accusing people when

137

you've got no proof. And you too, Tacky.'

The buzz faded down. It was not a night for disagreeing with Sanders who was standing treat all round.

'Nerissa!' Sanders called.

'Yes, suh?'

'Yes, suh? You old black cow, how much suh you give me las' night?'

'Las' night an' this night,' Nerissa said with surpassing dignity, 'is two totally different things.' She looked him squarely in the eye. 'You don' what I tell you. You don' sold that bit of land beside your house to Mister Miller.' Her voice rang with triumph.

'No,' Sanders said. 'I didn't sell it to Miller.'

'Then how you get all those dollars.'

'It's far too complicated for you to understand.'

'Mr Miller is a very complicated man.'

'Mr Miller is a prick.'

'A prick a very useful instrument.' She regarded him shrewdly. 'Not ebery t'ing wha' have sugar sweet. That what you saying, Mister Sanders? You come in with all those dollars but you look like crab wha' don' lose its shell. If you don' sell that bit of land to Mr Miller, who you sell it to?' She was burning with curiosity.

'Mind your own business.' He had had

138

enough of questioning. He looked down on Rosie.

'Fum fum now?' she said.

She restored his humour. He chuckled. 'How much you pay me?' It went over her head — she was a simple girl. 'Come on,' he said. 'Fum fum.'

She slipped off the stool in a twinkling and headed with alacrity for the stairs.

★ ★ ★

The rooms set apart for Nerrissa's girls were no more than wooden cubicles furnished with a single iron bed, a chair and clothes hooks; and so narrow that girl and client couldn't pass each other without their bodies touching. The conversion of the floor for prostitution had taken place when Nerissa had taken over what had once been The Shady Side Grocery when it lost its trade to the supermarket and she had simply gutted the upper floor and put in a central corridor with a staircase either end and doors on either side.

'This one ready,' Rosie said opening one of the doors — and where yesterday there had been a soiled sheet, today's was crisp and clean.

She undressed swiftly and without coquetry.

Naked she was small scale perfection — a well-arched back over buttocks as firm as a young boy's, flowering upturned breasts with distended nipples, a swan-like neck and slender limbs, coarse hair short and neat and ebony skin as smooth as the glazed cover of a book.

She lay down quickly on the sheet, her arms down by her side and legs apart, watching Sanders, finding him with his height and powerful hairy body satisfyingly masculine compared with most Antiguan men who, without being effeminate were, through the matriarchal history of generations of their background often womanly creatures. As she came to the bed she reached up her hand to the underside of his erect penis, soft and silky compared with the rest of him and stroked it gently. 'Him big and strong,' she commented. 'You like me Den-nis?'

'You little bitch,' he said. 'You beautiful little black bitch.' And he swung himself on to the bed, covering her — but by knees and elbows protecting her tiny body from his heavy weight as he entered her. At once her body, moist and ready, seized and closed about him. Seized and closed, contracted and released, while he stayed motionless. 'You delightful little whore,' he charged her. 'You fucking little harlot.

That's good. That's bloody good.'

He let her do the loving. She was amazingly adept with immense control of her vagina. Soft, strong, moist, elastic, her body talked to him and he fell silent answering with his own only with the first onset of climax when he took control and made love to her. Their bodies were utterly in tune because their minds were empty of both constraint and exaggeration; present sensuousness was the totality of their lovemaking and their shared climax while slow and steady in its coming was lasting in its being and wholly emptying in its effect. For the first time she felt the full crushing weight of him upon her and wriggled, wet with sweat, to ease from it.

'Sorry,' he apologised, 'but by God that was good.' He slapped her gently. 'You got best Soldier-Ring in business, Rosie.'

'You like me Den-nis?'

'I like you, Rosie. You number one fumming gal.'

'Why not I come live with you at Friendship?'

'Been working that one out, have you?' he said, but not unkindly. He was still within in her, held by her — she had merely eased enough to make the point he must take his own weight again. It was as if she was saying

141

she wouldn't let him go unless he agreed to her suggestion.

He thought about it, looking over the edge of the bed at the floor through the gaps in whose boards he could smell ganja and tobacco mingled and see splinters of light from the bar beneath. He could even hear the talk:

'*You is a bloomin' fool, Sylvester. Nex t'ing you saying is people try to work obeah on you make you do it.*'

'*No, man. I is not goin' to do it anyway. But I hearso . . .* '

'*Hearso make no pickneys!*'

'*Mister Sanders him busy making pickneys up there now.*'

This triggered off a gale of laughter and made Sanders smile.

'Them talking of we, Rosie,' he told her.

'H'm!' She injected tremendous scorn into the monsyllabic. 'Them only low count nygas.' She returned to the attack. 'If I come an' live with you at Friendship, you don' need to pay that wo'tless cruff you got. An . . . '

He stopped the beginning of a catalogue of reasons.

'I don't have no gal come an' live at Friendship, Rosie. I not one woman man.'

'You just don' tell me I got best Soldier-Ring in business.' And she gave his

142

flaccid penis a little tweak to underline her point.

'No,' he said. 'That's final, Rosie. But you can go on doing that and maybe soon I give it you again.'

His head was on the pillowless bed beside hers, his chin about brushing her hair, his body turned half sideways. Her sweat was strong with a different odour from his own. Outside a lorry passed rattling the timber frame; there was a mosquito somewhere in the room.

★   ★   ★

Later he gave her twenty dollars. 'Now this for you, Rosie,' he said. 'That not for Mistress Nerissa.'

She stopped pulling on her pedal pushers and sat back on the bed. She wore nothing underneath the pedal pushers and now they were in something of a scarlet tangle around the blackness of her limbs. 'Why not tell Mistress Nerissa where you got all that money, Den-nis?' she said.

'Because,' he told her, 'I've got to do some thinking first.' And, taking her partly into his confidence: 'There is a man who thinks him smart but him find out before him done him not so smart.'

'You don' like this man who give you all this money?' She found it difficult to believe.

'I intend,' said Sanders, 'to have his balls before I'm done.'

'Then you mus' have me come and live with you at Friendship.'

'How would that help?' He felt affectionate towards her: so miniscule, so childlike half-undressed, caught in the corner into which the bed just fitted.

'Because,' she said, her eyes big and flashing, 'although you a man and smart, Den-nis, woman is always smarter.'

Raleigh

When the tamarind had folded its leaves exposing a sky brilliant with countless stars seen through the fret of branches, Raleigh left his hut. But for the sound of insects the silence was total yet for a full five minutes he waited, listening. Once handsome but now made ugly after a cutlass fight in which he had lost an eye, not yet thirty he was in his prime: a man of huge strength, cunning, fearless and, above all, experienced.

At length, satisfied, he set off by first scaling a rough limestone outcrop and then made his way along a natural ledge over a difficult drop, a ledge which after a while turned abruptly and steeply downwards. The way was slippery but his feet were bare and he easily held his footing. He was dressed in tough black sailcloth slacks and a dark woollen jersey. He carried a machete blackened by paint except at its razored edge which glistened in the starlight. Crossed over one shoulder hung an old army knapsack. Quite soon soaked with moisture which brushed off every leaf and branch, he wound a tortuous path down amongst tree-shaded

145

rocks, through liana entanglements and the endless bush, yet moved with surprising speed and even more surprising silence. Every few minutes he would stop and listen — but there were only the sounds to which he was accustomed: the stir of leaves, the cicadas which paused around him as he moved leaving their own particular pool of silence, the guttural brown owl's cry, the pottoo who-hooing eerily.

Presently the bush began to yield and the slope to lessen and now he was low enough to see the first occasional mops of coconut palms silhouetted against the sky and the first bright twinkles amongst the thick growth which indicated distant houses. He broke through on to a rough marl track, deeply rutted with grass growing thickly on it. Here he waited for a full ten minutes and then cautiously, machete held out low ahead of him, he continued on his way until the track debouched on to one of the metalled roads of the San San subdivision. Swiftly crossing to one of the unsold lots from which he could see sections of the coast road winding its way below, the jutting lump of land which was Alligator Head and the necklace of the sea where it broke against the reef, he settled himself by a cottontree prepared for a lengthy vigil.

This was his favoured vantage point. He knew not merely the names of the owners of every house which he could see but their substances, whether they were in residence, the numbers and attitudes of their staffs, the precautions they took, whether they owned dogs and how difficult of access their properties were. All this intelligence he got from the local village, Drapers, where he would suddenly appear silently at night, machete in hand, and talk to the villagers by the smoky glow of Kelly lamps in wooden rum shops. He might stay for a night or two in a selected shack well back from the road from which he would vanish as silently as he had come. He had heard from them that the man named Mason who was to buy the Waterman's property had arrived and it was this which had tempted him from his lair: the easiest houses to rob were those occupied by visitors or new owners as yet unaware of the precautions they should take.

It was still early, scarcely ten o'clock, and there were lights winking brightly from several houses and the duller glows of yellow insect buzz-off bulbs on patios and balconies. Not infrequently a car twisted its way along the coast road, a moving double pencil of light appearing and disappearing in the trees, catching the sea like a lighthouse beam, vanishing behind a bluff. Occasionally one turned off the coast road as its owner returned from an evening away from home and Raleigh's eyes followed its headlights until they were switched off, noting which house it had reached. At last his patience was rewarded as he observed the lights of what had to be Mason's car searching upwards through the bush, saw them doused and replaced by a startling pool of brightness as the indoor house lights came on. Grunting with satisfaction, he lay the machete down beside him, leaned his back against a cottontree and fell asleep.

It was the treble discharge of Colonel Bannister's revolver which awakened him. He sat bolt upright, his hand instinctively reaching for the cutlass, his every nerve bristling with anticipation. But nothing followed to disquiet him, not even the nearby clanging which momentarily shattered the silence of the night; he knew exactly what that was: the alarm bell on 'Meiktila'. And because he knew the Colonel's habits, he knew that soon the Bannisters would be in bed. He lifted a massive hand and pulled his small beard thoughtfully. A glance towards the house Mason was renting proved that nothing could be done as yet for its lights were still burning brightly. But 'Meiktila?' Or, more to the point, that gun! He longed to own a gun. The possession of one was never far from his thoughts. If he owned a gun he would be able to steal from properties he'd never dared try stealing from before: houses with dogs — he hated dogs, you never knew where you were with them. With a gun he could shoot any that proved a nuisance. And if he was surprised, as he had once been, by a man with a revolver in his hand, why then he wouldn't be at a disadvantage. And, and this more important still, his prestige would be advanced. No one in the village would dare to cross or brook him if he owned a gun.

Overwhelmed by the sense of possible power he abandoned the idea of stealing from Mason's house. He must, he would have that gun. Unhurriedly he began to plan. There were still five hours of night to come; the gun would be in the Colonel's bedroom; he knew where that was because out of season he cased many of the San San properties. The bedroom was off the sitting-room. But there was no answer that way with too many locked doors to open and too much time for the Colonel to wake and be ready for him — and the Colonel, he had been told, was fearless.

For two long hours he wrestled with the problem, finding no answer while the traffic along the road became occasional, then rare;

while the stars shifted in their stations; while one by one the lights of the cottages went out until only the burglar lights remained. The breeze grew a little, chilling him through his dew-soaked clothes and his muscles began to cramp. At length, still undecided, still without a plan, as if drawn by a magnet he began to make his way cautiously to 'Meiktila', avoiding the patches of crisp, curled leaves blown by a recent Norther from the trumpet trees, seeking each scrap of cover, a silent shadow, wary, fearless, menacing.

Reaching the boundary, he kept within the shadow of the hibiscus hedge which ringed the property until he came to the driveway opening. The house stood, four-square, an island in a sea of cut bahama grass, an island lit at every corner of its roof by brilliant burglar lights. For minutes he stood staring at the swarms of insects flying around the lights, calculating the time it would take to cross a full thirty yards of lawn and the sounds he must make in doing so. By now he knew what he had to do: he had to kill the Bannisters, both of them if necessary. It was the only way to get that gun and he had to get it. The decision made he was calm. He had already killed a man and a man who has killed can kill again quite easily. The only question was how to achieve the killing with minimum risk.

It was Bannister who solved the problem. Bannister, who slept lightly, had served in Burma where he had won his Military Cross and, versed by jungle warfare, had learnt that tropical nights are only silent through good cause. And when Raleigh, making his move, had for all his stealthiness silenced the nearby bullfrogs and cicadas, Bannister who happened to be awake, was instantly alert. For long moments he lay listening, hearing nothing and then, very quietly so as not to disturb his wife, he slipped out from under his mosquito net, shoved his feet into his slippers, took the gun from off his bedside table, made his way out of the bedroom, crossed the sitting-room, opened a door and went out on to the patio. As Raleigh had heard, Bannister was a brave man — but he was also a proud and therefore sometimes a foolhardy man: a man who'd be damned if he'd allow intruders to sneak round his property unmolested.

At the side of the house, separated from it by a pathway, was the huge tank which supplied the house with water. Hearing the faint click of the opening door followed by the soft pad of feet, Raleigh slipped quickly behind its wall. Simple he might be but he was cunning and instinct told him what to do. In moments Bannister would pass between house and tank almost within touching

151

distance. Searching with his foot he found a loose piece of rock, quickly picked it up, then waited, rock in one hand, machete in the other. As he had anticipated Bannister having turned the corner of his house, revolver in hand, was making his way cautiously, almost soundlessly, along the path. When he was almost on him, Raleigh pitched the rock ahead of him. It was an old, old trick and in his Burma days Bannister might not have been deceived by it. But he was an old man now, his reactions less acute. His concentration momentarily distracted he took the fateful forward pace not looking to his left. It was enough. In a moment Raleigh was behind him, one arm around his chest, the other with the machete to his neck . . .

* * *

Joe Moseley, Jamaica's Minister of Tourism, got the news of Bannister's murder just after six that morning. The telephone didn't wake him for he was already up and about, in pyjamas and dressing-gown taking a leisurely stroll around the garden of his house. He heard the ring but although he hastened a little, his wife, Marcia, beat him to it and was answering the call as he stepped onto the patio where they always breakfasted.

'Hallo?' he heard. 'Yes ... Who wants him?' And, almost without a pause: 'That's Norman, isn't it? Norman ... ' it was lightly said, ' ... what the devil you doing, man, telephoning us this early? You think we got nothing better ... ' But she broke off and Joe, standing in the doorway, saw her expression change. 'Yes, he's here. No, you haven't woken him.' And from the change of tone, Joe Moseley knew it was something of moment.

He came in — an enormous, soft, generous, gentle man of mixed blood with thick pebbled glasses holding out a great ham of a hand for the instrument.

'Norman ... Yes, man, what is it?'

'There's been a murder over at San San, Joe. It happened about two this morning. I thought you ought to know.'

'Man if you're going to tell me ... '

'No, thank God, it's not von Thyssen or Prince Sadruddin. It's an Englishman named Bannister. One of our lesser San San residents — although a millionaire by all accounts.'

'What happened?'

'Damned arse tried to do our job for us. He must have heard the fellow who killed him and gone out to take a look.'

'Yes?'

'Damn fool went out with his gun and the fellow got him first. Cut his throat from ear to ear.'

'Holy Mother of God!' said Moseley. And, after a moment: 'Does Huie know?' Huie was the Prime Minister.

'Not yet.' The voice turned dry. 'I thought I'd leave that to you, Joe.'

'Remind me to do you a favour sometime.' But the quip was purely automatic : 'Anyone else hurt?'

'No.'

'Anything tiefed?'

'Just a gun. With six rounds in it.'

'Lawks!' said Joe. 'Now we're for it. Any idea who's got it?'

'Yes,' the Commissioner said. 'We think we know.'

'Raleigh?'

'Raleigh.'

'You'll *have* to catch him now.'

'Yes,' Norman Vair said. 'I rather think we *will* have to catch him now.'

'What have you done so far?'

'Set up road blocks between Hope Bay and Manchioneal. But that's only pyschological. If it's Raleigh, the last thing he'll do is leave the area.'

'Do you have to?'

'Set up road blocks? Yes. There's more to

Jamaica than your damn tourists.'

Joe Moseley thought about it for a while and then he said: 'What else you doing, man?'

'We're sending every available policeman to comb the mountains and we've asked for an Army helicopter.'

'And what do you think your chances are?'

'Of catching him this time? Evens maybe. Of catching him without someone else getting killed? Less than evens. Are you going over?'

Joe Moseley thought about it. 'No,' he said. 'No, I don't think so.'

There was a first chuckle from the other end. 'I didn't think you would . . . I'll keep in touch.'

'Do that, man, will you? . . . Oh, one other thing. Was he married?'

'Bannister? Yes.'

'How's she taking it?'

'Apparently very well.'

'Well, that's something.'

'Yes,' the Commissioner said. 'It's something. But it's not very much, is it?'

★ ★ ★

As Moseley put down the 'phone he found Marcia — a small woman with skin rather darker than his own and against him minute — looking up at him. A small woman but a decisive one who still considered him a child for all his political success. 'You're going to have a busy day,' she said. 'I'll hurry breakfast up.' And she went off to the kitchen, shouting to the cook.

Moseley went back into the bedroom, undoing the belt of his dressing gown. He switched on the radio but, discovering he was too late for the news, he went back into the hallway, the robe hanging loose and falling away from his enormous stomach, and dialled a number.

'Listen, man, have you got your Gleaner?' he demanded. 'No? Well we don't get it up here till half past seven. Will you do me a favour, man, and go and fetch yours.' While he waited he stared through the burglar bars at the rear covered patio where the table was already being laid and beyond it across the level garden which was cut off from the road by a hedge of neat plumbago. He noticed the sun picking up the parasites which, like lumps of hay picked from a passing cart, clung to the telephone wires.

A voice came on: 'It's in!'

'Damnation!' Joe Moseley said.

'You want me to read it to you?'

'No, it'll spoil my breakfast.'

'Do we see you at the Club today?'

'That,' said Joe Moseley, 'is a damn fool

question.' He heard the chuckle as he put down the receiver; then he picked it up again and dialled the Prime Minister.

★ ★ ★

The Gleaner arrived just as he sat down to breakfast. He heard the boy whistling up the drive, the splat of the paper thrown down on the hard tiled porch, the boy whistling his departure.

Marcia shouted: 'Beresford! Fetch the paper!'

Joe speared a slice of paw paw and squeezed lime juice over it; ahead of him the sun had already risen well above the plumbago hedge: nearby a doctor bird with its long black tails and emerald vest darted busily from scarlet hibiscus blossom to scarlet hibiscus blossom. Marcia poured coffee. It was just like any normal morning.

'What did he say then?' said Marcia, meaning Huie.

'That in the Chinese language the word *crisis* is made up of two characters: one meaning danger and the other opportunity.'

'Damn fool,' said Marcia.

'He didn't make it up, you know.' He said it mildly. He was concentrating on his paw paw and juice dribbled down his chin. He

157

reached for a serviette. He was back into dressing-gown and drawers after showering. 'It's serious. Damn serious.'

Beresford came out with the morning paper.

'Go and polish Mr Moseley's shoes,' Marcia ordered him, reaching for the paper.

'Leave the damn thing,' Joe said. 'Sweetheart, I beg you, leave it.'

'How long,' she rebuked him, 'you think I'm going to sit here waiting until you choose to tell me?'

He finished the paw paw, pushed the plate aside and leaned forward to inspect a dish of escovitched fish. He was so poor-sighted he had to lift his glasses and peer almost within touching distance.

'A Colonel Bannister,' he told her, letting the glasses slip back into place and helping himself to the fish, 'who had a house in San San got himself mashed by this man Raleigh they've been trying to catch for years and Raleigh tiefed his gun. And do you know who I've got to lunch at the Pegasus today? A party of American travel agents!'

* * *

He thought about it on the way down to the office. What a damn thing! What a damn hole

158

it was going to knock in this month's tourist arrivals. All that work! Harry Vivian in that damned expensive New York office selling white sand and limbo and Jamaican rum ... yes, and more to the point selling tranquillity and peace of mind. And that damned arse of a Raleigh and that damned arse of a Colonel Bannister between them will go and put the fear of God into the whole damn lot of them. If it had been in Kingston that wouldn't have been so bad. But a murder in San San where Princess Margaret had once stayed and where such internationally important people as Baron von Thyssen and Prince Sadruddin Aga Khan, and that Senator Holzer had built their holiday houses and God knows who else the glossies would dig up ...

He looked around him from the comfort of his chauffeur-driven air-conditioned Cadillac. Normally he enjoyed the drive down to his office; enjoyed the bustle, the noise, the converging of humanity as the requirements of another working day drained the higher, cooler areas, the modern flats, the cluttered shabby feeder lanes, mingling their occupants dispassionately, sending them south by private car, by bus, by cart, by bicycle, by foot, by donkey — sending them south to Kingston in a honking, shouting, bell-ringing, teeming mass of white, brown, black and yellow — but mostly black. He loved his country with a belly love of heat and blazing skies and strident colours and stench and noise and movement. And best of all he loved it at this hour when the heat had grown enough to dry away the dew but the promise of the day still lingered fresh and sparkling. Everything, he thought, heading hopefully south with him. South to Kingston: to New Kingston and old Kingston. Old Kingston — it was where his heart lay. In its old waterfront before the Matalons got busy redeveloping it, in the Myrtle Bank Hotel before they pulled it down, in the old Jamaica Club in the days of Bill Masterton and his like and lunch time liar dice on the old cracked marble table, in the area around Lady Musgrave Road, flat and hot and dusty, blue with vignum vitae blossom, mauve with bougeanvillea, vermilon with flamboyants. Old Kingston — once the only place to live. Things changed so quickly — and how much was it for the better?

They came to a halt in a traffic jam which seemed to stretch all the way to Mary Brown's Corner where the Mannings Hill traffic joins the Constant Spring Road. They stopped outside the market. Nowadays, apart from a handful of higglers still outside you had to peer into the gloom of a concrete cavern to know there was a market there at all but when he'd been a boy the cavern hadn't existed and the stalls of fruit and vegetables were stretched out in the open in a wondrous Persian carpet . . .

Magically the traffic jam dissolved and the stream moved swiftly southwards scarcely pausing again before Halfway Tree. But the mood had stayed with him. When I was a boy, he mused, what was here? The clear picture eluded him. The church? Yes. The tower? Yes. What else? Shacks, Chinese groceries, empty lots . . . But Kingston — now? Drive-in shopping centres, housing estates, a University, a College of Technology, hotels. He chuckled quietly. Oh, yes, hotels. Hotels of a quality undreamed of in those days. The old Myrtle Bank with all its atmosphere had been demolished, swept away because it wasn't the kind of hotel which yielded profit to the modern day holiday package operator. What he wanted was the standard ten storey high slab of a minimum two hundred rooms, preferably all identical so that one customer couldn't complain another had been better served. The two hundred room slab which utterly destroyed the charm of its location and spewed at fortnightly intervals four hundred tourists with bulging wallets and strident demands to be entertained and stole from the poor and simple villagers yet another white sand beach where once they had fished and loved and from which they were now excluded. And Joe Moseley, Jamaica's Minister of Tourism, thought about the tourists and wondered, and not for the first time either, where was the real profit in having them here at all.

★ ★ ★

'Good morning, Mr Moseley.'

'Good morning, my love.'

He liked all women but he liked the pretty ones best, the pretty and young ones. And Lelia was more than pretty — she was beautiful. Her skin was copper, her lips were full and sculptured into the slightest pout, her helmet of hair, long enough almost to touch her shoulders, was petal cut over dazzling eyes which were as jet black as her hair itself and were emphazised by the high cheekbones of her alert and intelligent face. She wore a white blouse over a pencil slim pale blue skirt; her breasts were high and very firm, her limbs superb; and when she moved, rarely hurriedly, it was utter poetry, head and shoulders back, a slight swaying of the hips and a projection of lazy sensualism. There was perfection in Lelia Thompson from head to toe and one of the high points of Joe Moseley's business days was this first morning reminder of her loveliness and sexuality. 'Man, I tell you, if once I got my hands round that lovely little arse, you'd have to prise them off!' But he had pebbled glasses, and a wife he loved. And he was Minister of Tourism. And he was sixty-two . . .

'Isn't it terrible Mr Moseley . . . '

'Darling, don't you worry your pretty head about it.' To take that pretty head between his hands, to kiss those pretty lips, to feel those pretty breasts against him. He sighed within himself. 'What's the post got to say, Lelia, my love?' He could only read the post by removing his glasses and holding it an inch or two from his eyes.. So he listened as she read the important letters and enjoyed the beauty of her lovely, lilting voice.

★ ★ ★

At about half past nine there was a telephone call from a man named Mason.

'All right,' Moseley heard Lelia say. 'I'll speak with him, Sylvia, if he's that insistent . . . Yes, Mr Mason . . . I'm his secretary . . . No, I'm afraid that just wouldn't be possible. He's got a very busy day . . . Hold on a moment, please.' And she was looking at him, a slender hand over the mouthpiece. 'It's a man named Mason. He wants to come and see you today.'

'Today! Doesn't the damn fool read the paper?'

'He says his time on the island's limited.'

He chuckled. 'Offer him an appointment two weeks today.'

Lelia's smile drew the taut coppery skin only the more smoothly over high cheekbones. She made no attempt to pass the message on. 'You know something, Mr Moseley,' she said. 'He's 'phoning from San San and he's talking about investing a few million dollars in a hotel there.'

'Put the gentleman on, my love,' he said.

* * *

'Mr Mason.' It might have been the call Joe Moseley had been eagerly awaiting all morning. 'What can I do for you?'

'I'd like to come in and see you this afternoon.'

'It's very short notice, Mr Mason.'

'Yes.'

Joe waited. He had an instinct for people — which was why he had got his Ministry.

164

When, he told himself, a man wanted urgently to see you and then held back his reasons he did so out of calculation. So he waited and, when nothing further was offered, repeated jovially: 'Very short notice.'

'Mr Moseley, I'm quite sure your secretary will have told you why I'm calling. And that my time on the island is very limited.'

He spoke as do men who are used to having their way — Moseley was nettled.

'Just a minute, Mr Mason,' he said — and played rather noisily with some desk papers. Lelia smiled. 'Yes, Mr Mason,' he resumed. 'You were saying?'

'I appreciate this is a difficult day for you.'

Ah. So he knows. Well, of course he would. That's why he's phoning.

'Yes, Mr Mason, it is.'

'Mr Moseley, I'm 'phoning from San San and it is precisely because of what has happened here that I would like to come and see you.'

'It isn't something we can talk about over the telephone?'

'Minister. I am on the point of signing a contract to buy a property in San San for over two million American dollars and I have been considering investing an even larger sum in a new hotel locally. I have to leave for New York tomorrow to set up the operation. If, before I

165

leave, I cannot get the reassurances I need — and which it is reasonable I should have — I shall not be proceeding with either project. I think you must understand what I am talking about and that it is hardly a matter which could be dealt with on the telephone.'

His instincts telling him that he had skewered out of Mason a good deal more than he had originally intended to divulge over the telephone, Moseley felt better-humoured. 'Of course not, Mr Mason,' he said agreeably and, glancing at a far from full diary: 'I can offer you between four and four-fifteen this afternoon. On the other hand . . . '

'I will be with you, Mr Moseley at four precisely.'

★ ★ ★

Joe Moseley leaned back in his comfortable chair.

'My love,' he said to Lelia, who made the day so much more pleasant by sharing his large office with him and had to be there anyway to be his eyes, 'what reassurances do you think a man thinking of spending two million *American* dollars . . . ' he stressed the adjective ' . . . on a house in San San and several million more on a local hotel would be

166

expecting to get from the Minister of Tourism to persuade him to go on with it?'

'It can't be only to do with the murder, can it?' she replied, 'I mean, any man who's got that sort of money has to know that security is a matter for the police.'

'Unless,' Joe said sagely, 'he has such a low opinion of our policemen, he believes he has to get the Government to hurry them up!' He picked up his telephone: 'Sylvia, my love, get me Mr Betty, will you?' And when Betty came through, after pleasantries about the man's wife who hadn't been well: 'Well, Max that's good news. Give her my love, won't you. Now, Max, will you do something for me. There's a man in San San, Mason, an Englishman by the sound of him, who's thinking of buying a house there for two million American dollars and investing a lot more in a hotel. I want you to find out everything about him and let me know by three at the latest what you've discovered. That won't be difficult, will it, man?'

'Not difficult at all, sir.'

Joe put down the telephone. 'Lelia, my love, have you ever been to San San?' And at the brief shake of her head, teasingly: 'The most beautiful part of Jamaica and you've never been?'

'Never.'

'I rather think,' he said, ' that is a negligence which must be rectified before too long.'

★ ★ ★

Norman Vair was greatly impressed by Dora Bannister — and Dora Bannister was impressed by Norman Vair. He had feared to find an hysterical woman who, sufficiently recovered, would rail against local security and be of no help at all. But Dora Bannister's love for her husband had been so deep that even in his death he gave her strength and she behaved much as if he was alive, advising her.

'Come in, Inspector,' she invited him.

He entered, tall and erect, neat in spotless khaki shorts and bush-jacket with a shiny leather belt and carrying a cane. His shoes were blacker and shinier than his face and his long socks impeccably straight. He wore a peaked cap which he removed on entering.

She led him through a sitting-room so square and starkly furnished as to convey more the feeling of a hall and out to the flat tiled patio overhung by a heavy, concrete canopy. But if artistically the house was a total failure, its view was spectacular and especially so in the mornings when the sun shafted huge green shadows from each mountain range on to its neighbour. There was tremendous majesty in these deep, soft-looking, crystal-clear, green mountain folds in the sharp morning light, a huge finality in the crisp lines of their summits, a satisfying mystery in their shadowed valleys and altogether, with nowhere a scar with the forest so flooding the harsh limestone rock as to turn it all to velvet, an overall perfection.

'We'll sit out here, Inspector,' she instructed him. He bowed assent and as she settled her enormous bulk billowing in an ankle-length, small-patterned, navy-blue dress he placed his cap and cane on the nearby table. He watched her clasp her hands and rest them in her lap and noticed how her hair, fine and grey, trailed an odd wisp in the breeze.

'I'm sorry,' he said, 'to put you through an inquisition at such a time.'

'It has to be done.'

'Yes. I have little to ask at the moment but there will be a detective coming to interview you later.'

She realised that this was really only a courtesy visit.

'We all know it was Raleigh,' she said.

'It was most likely Raleigh.'

She liked his dignity, his unhurried delivery, his respectful yet utterly self-assured manner. She appreciated his coming without an entourage, with only the one policeman sitting stiffly in the car outside. Arthur, she told herself, would have approved.

'I can tell you very little, Inspector,' she said. 'I was awakened by a sound which was, I have come to believe, my husband's revolver falling on the path. Then I heard other sounds . . . ' She paused, controlling herself, making a motion of denial with a substantial hand as if to head off words of comfort. 'I didn't hear anything else after that, I was making too much noise getting out of bed and I don't move very fast and I had the mosquito net to deal with before I could switch on a light. Then I saw Arthur had gone and I went to the window and through the open jalousies I saw him lying on the ground.' Her tongue touched her upper lip but otherwise she showed no emotion. She had, he realised, schooled herself to face what had to be said and done and he guessed her grief would be the worse for it when he had gone and there was no longer any purpose in controlling it.

'Was it you?' he asked, 'who switched the alarm bell on.'

'No. I think it must have been Phyllis.

Hyacinth was too hysterical to know what to do.'

'And how long would you say . . . '

'Two or three minutes.'

'And all that time . . . '

'I was with my husband. I knew he was dead. I knew there was nothing I could do for him.'

His heart went out to her in the horror of her recollection: the eyes in the half-dismembered head staring at her, his warm blood soaking through her nightdress. He was grateful for the doorbell ring.

'No,' she said, her hand restraining him. 'Phyllis will go. Is there anything else?'

'Did you hear anything at all while you were with your husband? Footsteps? A car? Anything?'

'I heard nothing.' It was firmly said — said firmly to shut out the sounds she would never forget: the sounds of a man being butchered.

Norman Vair was moved. Death was no stranger to him but there was something so heroic in Mrs Bannister's way of facing up to this ghastly business as to intensify the tragedy. He was glad to see her eyes light up as she struggled to her feet.

'That's Mr Cusack,' she said. 'How nice of him to call.'

Dora Bannister held out her hand to Freddie Cusack — a man in his early fifties, an American from the middle west, with fine, soft, white hair and a deeply lined forehead, with a big nose over a clipped moustache, with receptive, intelligent, kindly eyes under bushy brows.

'How kind of you to come,' she said.

The Commissioner had gone and apart from a few local idlers lounging by the gate, open-mouthed yet apprehensive as if nervous Raleigh might suddenly dart out from the bush, one would have had no idea that this morning at 'Meiktila' was different from any other. Hyacinth, albeit with shaking hands, was hanging washing on the line, Phyllis was sweeping up last night's collection of dead insects and Rupert, the garden boy, was sweeping up leaves: trumpet leaves, mango leaves, almond leaves, star apple leaves, pimento leaves — and pitching them on to the adjacent unbought vacant lot. A liver coloured lizard which had watched the murder taking place was hiding behind the alarm bell leaving the blinding daylight to his more vivid daytime fellows; such night moths as had escaped being eaten by the logger-heads had mysteriously vanished; the John

Crows were circling lazily. There were a few people on the private beach owned by the San San residents and had you looked at them through Colonel Bannister's extraordinarily powerful telescope you would have noticed how unusually close together they were.

'I didn't know,' Cusack said, 'if I could be of any use or if you'd even want anyone around but I just couldn't not come, Mrs Bannister.'

'Mr Cusack,' she replied, 'there is no one in San San I would prefer to see this morning but you should not have come all the way you have. There is nothing you can do to help, nothing anyone can do.'

'You would be more than welcome . . .'

'No,' she interrupted firmly.

'With you being up here alone I shan't rest easy in my mind . . .'

Again she interrupted, glancing down at the knots of men and women on the beach far down below: 'There will be many people who will not be easy in their minds, Mr Cusack. But there is nothing to worry about now. There are police all around the place.' She looked away from the beach and up to the mountains, now less soft, the green more aggressive in the dazzling light. 'Some-where up there most probably,' she said, 'is a man with my husband's blood still on him. I've tried to imagine what he's feeling like but I can't manage it. Because I don't know what he's like and the way people feel when something happens to them depends on what they're like inside themselves. And we're not even Jamaicans, Mr Cusack. We're English and Canadian and American and German and heaven knows what else. And we come and spend three months or so in houses we have built to escape the worst of our winters and then when spring comes we go home again and although the people we know at home mostly imagine that after coming here year after year we must have got to know Jamaicans well, they're quite wrong. What Raleigh, if it is Raleigh, as it probably is, what Raleigh up there is thinking, feeling, imagining, I can't begin to guess. They say he's fearless . . .'

She broke off at a new and distant sound, an unusual sound for San San.

'That's a helicopter coming, Mr Cusack, isn't it?' she said.

He nodded. 'Yes, Mrs Bannister, that's a helicopter.' And he turned his head to follow its approaching path.

'I don't know about fearless, Mrs Bannister,' he said. 'But if Raleigh is up there from a minute or two now on he's going to be a very frightened man.'

★　★　★

Cusack was right. It had never occurred to Raleigh before that anything could frighten him except the spirits in the bamboo groves and the duppies in the silk-cotton trees. But the helicopter frightened him and here he was this proud, strong Koramantee crouching down, daring only to look over his shoulder at it every time it passed. His fear was greater than that of a hunted animal because knowledge was added to apprehension. The helicopter was not a hunting bird but a carrier of men searching for him with eyes as sharp as those of the red-tailed hawk; with eyes perhaps even sharper; with eyes, which, for all he knew, had some secret way of piercing the flimsy screen of leaves protecting him. And whenever the helicopter passed close enough he saw the way the branches swayed and parted, opening blue strips and segments in the sky and he felt as naked as if the hills were suddenly a desert.

After killing Bannister, he had seized the gun and forgotten stealth, the nature of his crime transcending everything. At once exultant, awed and irresolute, his normal cunning overmastered, rather than picking his path with care he had forced his way directly through all impediments and by the time the agitation in his mind had calmed enough for him to pause and review the situation blood from a dozen unnecessary cuts was mingled on his body with his victim's. By then he had covered halfway back to the beginnings of his ledge, a half littered with clumsy indications which he knew would point like an arrow towards his lair. There was, he saw, only one solution; he must create a false trail to some place with several points of exit from which he would choose one and then, with exquisite care, withdraw and by a circuitous route make his way back to the hut. Then, as evening approached, he would dismantle it and, under the shelter of the night, make his way to the second of his three retreats: a place in the mountains between Ecclestown and Fishbrook where the steady north-east trades so filled the air with moisture that there was rarely escape from the swirling mists and rain-filled clouds. No one would find him there, it was too inhospitable. He would rest up for a week or two, snaring birds and existing off the land and the small supplies he would carry with him. Then, finally, he would move further eastwards still, to his third hut above Muirton within reach of friends.

But the plan must wait till dawn. Even Raleigh, for all his intimate understanding of this wild, jagged country, dared not risk a blind, unknown path in the night which might suddenly end in a precipice masked by overgrowth. So, soaked with sweat and dew, shivering with the cold, he had possessed himself in patience, awaiting dawn.

★ ★ ★

It came at last with its fantastic, simultaneous switch off of a million cicadas and the foliage turning grey, then green and the sky seen through gaps in it colouring yellowish with coppery clouds above pale blue to the east and pearl with pink and grey above Port Antonio to the west.

Raleigh made his move until he came upon a place where there was no obvious choice of direction and here, turning westwards, away from his hut, he began to cut a cutlass path where the undergrowth was thick. It was gruelling work and the going slow except in rare places where some ceiba or saman so withheld the sun as to inhibit growth. He pushed his way through nets of mixed convolvulus and spiders' webs, stumbled on fallen trunks of primeval trees the black mould of their casings sprouting forests of moss and ferns, gutless, wet as sponges, crumbling at his touch. He scaled green-mossed rock faces and slithered down soaking slopes, lowering himself hand after hand by doubtful branches and ropes of vines. He was pricked by spiny thorns and rocks and branches scraped and sliced his skin re-opening night wounds which had begun to heal. His satchel caught and hindered him, the gun inside it banged and bruised his back, his sweat flowed in rivers from every pore and into every crevice of his body and as the sun grew stronger and with it the humidity and heat, his breath became an agony. But he struggled on, a terrible sight to see, blood and sweat and filth, torn clothes, scarred face, one staring eye and a blackened machete scything in his hands.

At last this crucifying industry was rewarded. He found himself of a sudden in an open glade of lofty tree ferns, windless, eerie, silent, dappled with the glow of sunlight shafting through, diffused to pale gold and painting the myriad greens of ten million leaves in curious, lovely, delicate arabesques. He paused and rested, panting, lying on his back, the machete cast a yard or two away. He had gone, he reckoned, far enough.

★   ★   ★

It was about midday when the helicopter awakened him with its ugly, exploding,

178

knocking sound. He got quickly to his feet, his eyes following the movement of the invisible machine but not immediately relating it to himself. Stirred to new effort by its presence, he looked about him, decided, and then choosing an opening in the surrounding bush forced a path through it, cutting a way for perhaps ten minutes until it thinned again offering several choices. He chose two of these, going as far again in each case, leaving less obvious signs and then withdrawing from both and returning with great care to the glade. It was now he made his exit, backing and carefully rebuilding in front of him a small stockade masking his departure point. It was slow, arduous, artistic work and in an hour he managed perhaps ten or fifteen yards but even a skilled tracker would not have known a man had left the glade that way.

*   *   *

Through the long afternoon, the helicopter haunted him as he circled slowly and carefully back to his normal path to reach it well above the place where he had left it. Having realised by now he was its quarry he knew the fierce frustration of a man who spends an hour covering a distance a machine can cover in seconds and he was sorely tempted to abandon the idea of returning to his hut at all. But it held his few provisions, his tobacco, ganja and the small thefts which were his capital. And it was *there* — the most carefully selected and therefore most secret and convenient hiding-place of all. In fact, his home. If he didn't dismantle and hide every vestige of it, he would never be able to use that place again.

★ ★ ★

By the time he regained the track, to manage the balance of a journey which would normally have seemed nothing to him, now seemed a Sisyphean problem. But he fought his weariness. The beginning of the last climb where the slope was steep and like a Jacob's ladder all but defeated him but afterwards it was easier. Once on the ledge he was exposed and he guessed that its very formation must attract the helicopter's interest. And so it evidently did. Time and again he was forced to hide at its approach. Concealing himself in undergrowth or at times pulling down branches to cover himself, he peered at it through orifices and was able to see the pilot and the watching crew. His soul was filled with hatred and his mind with a kind of fear he had never visualised. But at last, exhausted, he reached his goal and even in his continuing apprehension knew the triumph of success and the comfort of being back amongst his few possessions.

It had been in vain. Three hours before he gained his refuge, the hut had been discovered and reported.

★ ★ ★

'Norman!' Joe Moseley said indignantly. 'In about ten minutes I've got a man coming to see me who's thinking of putting a lot of money into an hotel at San San and will want to be reassured his guests wont be murdered in their beds. And you suggest I tell him he can go straight ahead because you think the man who chopped up Colonel Bannister is in a hut by Nonsuch! Rass, man! What sort of crazy suggestion is that you're giving me?'

'I didn't,' chuckled Vair, on the other end of the telephone, 'suggest you did. I said that's where we think Raleigh is.'

'But Nonsuch!'

'Well you can say Sherwood Forest if you prefer. It's about equidistant between the two.'

'Nonsuch! Sherwood Forest! I wonder who the hell it was chose all these damn fool names for all these places. You think Mason'd believe a word of it. Anyway, what makes you think he's there?'

'The helicopter spotted a hut with a bit of a clearing in front of it on the edge of a ravine that's too steep even for a goat to manage. And they've caught glimpses of him heading for it through the day.'

'Can you get to it?'

'The hut? Yes. There's a ledge above it that's interrupted by a rock fall. We've got two parties going to seal the ledge at either end. If he's in the hut there's no way he can get away.'

'Why not down into the ravine?'

'It's all but vertical.'

'There's no room to land the helicopter?'

'No.'

'Are you using dogs?'

'No, they'd get excited and he'd hear them.'

'He'll hear you anyway.'

'I doubt it. When the parties get near enough — which should be in about an hour's time — the helicopter's going to stick around making enough of a racket to put the fear of God into him and cover any other sound. It's just landed back on the Boston strip to refuel and 'll be setting off again in about ten minutes. The men'll be in striking position at both ends of the ledge about fiveish. They'll move in at dusk.'

'Why not earlier? He might give you the slip.'

'No, man! He's got a gun with six rounds in it and I'm not having my men taking a bigger risk than they have to. And if he is in the hut there's no way he can get away. He's either got to scale this damn great lump of rock and have us waiting for him or go down the slope which is impossible without a ladder.'

'And if he isn't in the hut?'

'Well, Joe,' said Norman Vair, 'I'm open for suggestions.'

★　★　★

'I think, my love, we will mention none of that to Mr Mason.'

'Why not, Mr Moseley?'

'Because the man's got a helluva reputation as a slick operator who comes out on a profit in the deals he's mixed up in while everyone else gets hurt. Best play sister peel-head fowl and give him less to hit us with later on.' He tapped the folder on the desk meaningfully. 'Betty's done a damn good job. Listen to this.' He took off his glasses and picking out the top sheet from the folder held it close to his eyes jiggling it all the time to get the parts he wanted to read out into focus. 'No,' he said, 'You read it.'

He handed her the sheet and she read out aloud. 'Derek Richard Mason. Aged fifty-one. Born in England but now a Bahamian subject. Specializes in promotion of tourist projects in which he retains control through careful and imaginative use of local situations. Recent developments include the White Reefs Hotel in Tobago in which all the original stockholders lost their money and Mason successfully defended himself against a conspiracy to defraud and the Beach Resort in Bermuda which ground to a halt through being underfinanced and was bought up later at a knockdown price by a company in which Mason had a hands-off interest.'

'Doesn't sound the sort of man you'd invite to join your poker school, does he, my love?'

'Sounds like a hurry-come-up to me,' said Lelia seriously — and read on: 'Mason is currently negotiating to buy a house called Petrea in San San through a Panamanian company he controls. The interesting thing about Petrea is that its owner, a Canadian named Waterman, has an option to purchase Lutman's Haven which is a shabby little bungalow set in half a dozen acres of coconuts running down to a white sand beach four or so miles east of San San on which planning approval has been given for a hotel of the Plantation Inn style.' She handed back the sheets to Moseley: 'Well!' she said with feeling.

Moseley smiled: 'The thing I like about Betty,' he chuckled, 'is his brevity. But, you, my love, do even better.'

Lelia thought for a moment. 'The last thing,' she observed, 'the Jamaican tourist industry can do with just now is another catastrophe like we had on the Arawak Hotel!'

'And this man Mason sounds just the kind of fellow to give us one.'

'Doesn't he?' And leaning back in her chair in an attitude which made Joe Moseley in spite of the love he had for his wife wish he was twenty years younger and an impish smile which demonstrated the accord there nevertheless was between them: 'Perhaps we ought to ask Inspector Vair to take things easy and let Raleigh get away.'

Joe smiled ruefully. 'Too late, my love. When rock starts tumble down hill, him not stop until him reach bottom.'

★   ★   ★

185

Mason, carrying a slim leather briefcase and wearing a lightweight, impeccably cut, if rather aggressive tropical suit over a shirt of fine cotton and an expensive silk designer's tie, proved to be a man of middle height, with smooth dark hair and a neat moustache, steel-rimmed glasses and a resolute smile which displayed a set of teeth which looked a trifle too perfect for a man of his age.

'How kind of you to make time to see me, Mr Moseley,' he said withdrawing the perfectly-manicured hand which had momentarily been lost in Moseley's huge paw. 'Especially when you must have so much on your mind.'

Moseley smiled and, indicating the chair across the desk from his own said: 'Please.'

Mason seated himself after dropping the briefcase on the corner of the desk — an action which Moseley found too self-sufficient and faintly irritating.

'You have a very beautiful island, Mr Moseley,' Mason essayed. 'And a very interesting one. I came into Kingston via Port Morant and that's the first time I've done that drive and I found it quite unforgettable.' And he went on for a little while mentioning one or two things he'd seen en route which he'd found particularly fascinating.

I wonder which guide-book he got half of

that from, Moseley mused while managing to project an air of being gratified his visitor should have been so impressed but strictly limiting his own responses. In any case he was at something of a disadvantage in that he had only once driven to San San via Port Morant and that many years ago. Kingston was Joe Moseley's Jamaica — he was quite happy to pass on the North Coast to the tourists.

Mason in fact needed a space in which to form his judgement of his host. A man who ahead of a meeting liked to do his homework thoroughly, he was irked that the Raleigh business had obliged him to cut corners. Moreover, having assumed Moseley would be black, he had been a trifle thrown to find he wasn't. But the distraction was only momentary. Inclined to expatiate on the necessity of self-discipline and self-control in order to achieve a goal, he found Moseley gross and unimpressive. He read the affability as that of someone unsure of himself and the fact that the man was clearly half-blind, far from engaging his sympathy made him wonder what on earth the Jamaican Government was thinking of doing to choose as its Minister of Tourism a man as limited as this Moseley had to be. But then, he reminded himself, Jamaica was a limited place and limited places spawned limited people. Most likely he had got where he was through nepotism — until independence at least, as his researches had informed him, most of those who wielded commercial power throughout the Caribbean had had a Middle Eastern background watered down through intermarriage.

He adjusted his planned approach — the emphasis must be on the commercial benefit he was offering.

'Well, I mustn't ramble on,' he said and giving a little nod towards Lelia who was busying herself filing letters. 'I wonder . . . '

'You don't have to worry,' Moseley responded firmly.

Mason accepted defeat. 'Good.' He unzipped the brief case in a brisk and decisive movement, took out a two or three page document and then managing to convey a slight interruption to his flow with a smile clearly intended to confirm an understanding between them: 'But of course this all has to be kept sub rosa.'

Moseley (who was finding his preconception justified by every moment that passed) nodded gravely and called warningly: 'You hear that, Lelia?'

'Yes, Mr Moseley.'

Mason secretly doubting if the girl understood the term, held up his document and said, 'This is an option I have to buy a San San property which includes a six acre beach site. It expires at six p.m. tomorrow.' He looked through the enormously thick glasses into the Jamaican's eyes as if determined if need be to stare him out. 'My interest,' he said — making a positive statement clearly not to be denied — 'is in developing this site into a major tourist hotel for which I need hardly tell you there is a great need in the San San area.'

'You are of course talking about Lutman's Haven,' Moseley said, deciding it appropriate not to appear completely uninformed. 'We have given the owner, Mister . . . ,' He glanced questioningly at Lelia.

'Mr Waterman,' she supplied.

'Waterman,' Moseley agreed. 'Yes. We have given him approval for a fifty room hotel there.'

Mason gave a small and somewhat contemptuous laugh. 'But, Minister,' he said destructively, indeed almost insolently, 'you cannot possibly waste such a magnificent beach on a fifty bedroom hotel!'

A riposte in Jamaican vernacular which might have warned Mason he was misreading the character of the man across the desk from him, flashed through Moseley's mind. With a little difficulty he

189

resisted making it and said instead: 'What are you proposing, Mr Mason?'

'Well at least three hundred rooms. Possibly even more.'

'Three hundred!' cried Moseley, glad to take refuge in apparent enthusiasm.

'I have,' Mason (calculating that if his previous involvement in the Caribbean was not already known to his host, it must be sooner or later) went on with a positiveness again not to be denied, 'considerable expertise in developing hotels. For example the White Reefs in Tobago was one of mine. You've heard of it?' And, at Moseley's nod: 'We had a little trouble there.' He smiled self-reproachfully. 'I was rather lacking in experience at the time.' He shrugged it off. 'But I learnt a great deal from it and especially that one of the vital ingredients of a successful tourist promotion is retaining the confidence of those investing in it. Which of course brings me to my reason for asking you to give up your valuable time to see me. I have set up a meeting in New York the day after tomorrow with an American who heads a group interested in an hotel investment here. If I am still interested in proceeding, I intend to offer him the opportunity of participating in . . . ' he gave the document a shake ' . . . this. But as I am sure you must realise, Colonel Bannister being murdered has thrown the whole project into doubt.'

'But Mr Mason,' Moseley objected, 'I can't see why the situation is so very different today from yesterday. Everyone in San San has known about that rascal for years . . . '

'But then,' interrupted Mason, 'he didn't own a gun and that, I assure you, Mr Moseley, makes a great deal of difference.'

Moseley resisted the temptation of saying he failed to see why — that it was just as unpleasant having one's throat cut by a machete as being shot.

Mason went on: 'The immediate effect of what happened in San San last night must be to lower confidence in the area and I am not prepared to enter into a contract until I am able to reassure investors that it will be safe for people to stay in their hotel.'

'I can promise you,' said Moseley feigning eagerness, 'that the police will be doing everything possible to catch the fellow.'

'Everything *they* can,' Mason agreed. 'But will that be enough? I have only until tomorrow evening to exercise my option and the fellow has been a local menace they've been trying to catch for years and utterly failing to do so. And that was even before he owned a gun. No, Mr Moseley with great respect I submit that this is far too important a matter to be left purely to the police.'

'So what are you suggesting, Mr Mason?'

'I realise that I am presuming a great deal when I say this,' Mason said coolly, 'but, bearing in mind that a major boost to your tourist industry depends on a successful outcome to this matter, I am suggesting the military be called in. It is the only way you can be sure of catching him.' He got abruptly to his feet and putting his papers away ended rather dramatically: 'I am in your hands, Mr Moseley. That murderer must be caught and caught quickly. If by this time tomorrow he is still at large with a loaded revolver in his possession, then I shall not be taking up that option and the Jamaican tourist industry will be the loser. Thank you for your time. Good afternoon.'

He gave the briefest of nods to Lelia and was gone.

★　★　★

Abandoning her pretence of filing, Lelia moved unhurriedly and gracefully across the room to stand facing Moseley across his desk

'Well, man?' she said.

He was grateful. To address a Government Minister thus was only a shorthand way of expressing her understanding of Moseley's efforts through the interview and suggest he unburdened himself.

With her slim body almost within reaching distance, her coal black brilliant eyes holding his own and the perfume she used stirring his senses, Moseley could have obliterated the rankling Mason had left in him by taking her in his arms. But a desk lay between them — and forty years. And something more: the belief that promises should be kept, that without the strength to hold to his loyalties, a man was nothing.

'Mason's a shit,' he said.

She understood that too. Moseley did not use such words in front of women. Through the year and more she had been employed by him he had never done so before. Doing so now was to answer her question fully. It said it all. She let it pass. 'Check!' she said. Then abruptly changed the emphasis and went back to her own desk.

'Obviously,' she said, while doing so, 'he must have left for Kingston before the helicopter got busy.' She sat down and faced him. 'Why didn't you *tell* him about it. He'll find out as soon as he gets back to San San.'

'I doubt,' he replied, 'if he'll be going back there tonight.'

'But even so?'

'Did you ever,' he replied circuitously, 'hear

any man so damn facety?'

'You didn't like Mr Mason, did you,' she chuckled.

'Did you?'

She shook her head. 'I don't know how you controlled yourself.'

'Well,' he replied with a grin, 'you never call alligator long mouth till you pass him.' But the goodhumour was short-lived. 'What sort of fellow, is that?' he demanded. 'Didn't give a cuss about poor old Bannister.'

'Or his wife.'

'Or his wife. Only thing he's interested in is that damn option.'

'I wonder how much he had to pay for it.'

'Yes,' agreed Moseley, not without satisfaction. 'I wonder.'

'And then there's that house he's thinking of buying. Petrea. Whatever he was going to pay for it, it can't be worth that much now.'

'And if he buys it, he'll have to sleep in it.'

'With maybe a murderer with a gun pencilling Petrea in for his next tieving!' Her eyes were sparkling. 'Did he strike you as likely to be brave enough?'

'He didn't strike me as another Colonel Bannister.'

She thought for a moment and then said: 'But if they catch Raleigh today there isn't any way you can stop him exercising that option, is there? And no reason on earth why he shouldn't. And they are going to catch Raleigh, aren't they? Anyway there isn't any good reason for objecting to a three hundred bedroom hotel being built near San San, is there?'

He peered at her through his thick glasses. 'There are times, my love,' he observed, 'when instinct is a better guide than reason. And I have a gut feeling that in the long run Jamaica will be a damn sight better off if Mason doesn't exercise that option.'

'You're not thinking of having a word with Inspector Vair?' she chided him.

He seemed to take it seriously. 'A murderer can kill one man, maybe two, but a crook can destroy a thousand.' He tapped the document Betty had prepared. 'I'm not sure that a man like Mason isn't more dangerous to Jamaica than a dozen Raleighs.' He sighed. 'But no, my love, I'm not going to have a word with Vair. And if I did, he wouldn't give a blast.' He glanced at his watch. 'Anyway, it's just about now, he'll be going in for the kill.'

★   ★   ★

It came as a huge relief to Raleigh when the helicopter moved away — his ears were buzzing and his head ached from the sound of it. He was stiff and cramped, his belly nagged him, his wounds were stinging, his thirst was terrible. It was the first thing he attended to, his thirst, when he regained the hut. Then, having done so, he set about demolishing his lair.

Organised and practised, he cut the vines intelligently and re-used them to rebind the thatch into a parcel, working very quickly with the sun already dipped behind the ridge of a nearby hill. It was far from dark but was that time of a tropical day when, on the lowlands, the sun seems to pause as if reluctant to sink while it still has strength. But here the day lingered with a different light and mood. There were no shadows and dimensions weakened as a hundred different greens faded into one and then that to grey. The brightness which remained was that seen through the rain tree as it began to fold its leaves together as night approached. To the west the orange glow grew vivid and it was when it had become like the sky above a fired city that Raleigh heard the sounds. He was about to tie into a bundle a batch of rafter poles when he heard the sudden thudding of a rock, bouncing and tearing through the undergrowth of a nearby slope. He paused finding this strange because although after rain this was a sound he was used to hearing, there had been no rain since the last Norther ended. And next, alerted even more than normally, he heard branches rustling unnaturally and the sudden irritable cry of a bird disturbed. He stood, his body taut, his eye a bright gleam in the gathering gloom, aware he was discovered, judging the distance and likely number of his enemies, calculating which of his few possessions he still had time to gather and take with him. His only thought was flight. It did not occur to him to use his gun. That had been a misreading by Norman Vair — to Raleigh the gun was far more a talisman than a weapon. Surprised whilst robbing, he might have used it; that would have been instinct. But the instinct now was flight and, if he failed to elude his captors, it would be his cutlass and his strength.

Abandoning his half-dismembered hut, he began, selectively, to fill his satchel and then a sack, pausing often to listen, confident he could outwit his enemies. After a time the sounds ceased and, reading this correctly — that they would wait until it was all but dark — he threw back his head and laughed. He would have ample time to make his escape — to get to him they would have to scale the rock fall first.

When the sack was filled he tied it at the neck and going to the edge of the cleared slope he released it and watched it as it tumbled noisily until far away, down at the bottom it was stopped by undergrowth. The sound of it, as he had anticipated, brought about renewed activity from his would-be captors and for the first time he heard whispering. It was time to go. Slipping the satchel over his shoulder, machete in hand, he began to scale the rock intending to escape through a fissure of which his enemies would be unaware existed and then make his way along the ledge in the opposite direction from which the muffled voices had come, circle round and down, retrieve his sack and be off through the dense bush into safety. At night, an army itself, would fail to find him in the fastness of these high John Crow Mountains.

One-handed, he climbed, his machete in the other, a menacing silhouette against the fading eastern sky. The voices were louder now, no longer muffled. They had heard his move. An order was barked, and answered, and there came the scrabbling sound of climbing feet. Raleigh was untroubled: he knew the easiest way and it would take him less time to reach the ledge than it would for his pursuers to scale the rock fall. Reaching the fissure he made his way through it, careless now of any sound he made. He heard a cry: 'Look out, Henderson, he's on the move!' The strength and direction of the voice puzzled him but when it rang out again: 'Are you there, man? Answer me?' and a voice as loud called back: 'Yes, sir! We're in position!', he understood. They had loud-hailers and were on either side — he was pincered on the rock.

He froze, listening.

'He's stopped!'

Nothing could have been more threatening — that they could read his movements, or lack of movements, so distinctly.

And, as if they read his mind, at once he heard a voice addressed to him, a West Indian voice drilled out of the vernacular for circumstances such as these:

'Listen to me, Raleigh. We know exactly where you are. Both ends of the ledge are covered. You can't get away so dont make you situation worse. Now answer me! Do you give yourself up or do we have to come down to fetch you? I repeat! Do you give yourself up or do we have to come down to fetch you.' There was a pause and then the same voice called: 'Henderson, he seems to have stopped. Do you make it that he's stopped?'

'I can't hear him moving, sir!'

'Right, then. Carry on!'

The voices were echoing through the fissure. Raleigh could not imagine how they had got so close to him undetected on this end of the ledge.

'Raleigh!' he heard, 'do this! Keep going the way you were. Through that cleft. Be warned that there are men with rifles trained on it where it opens out. And soldiers trained on the rock the other side.' The voice was echoing strangely, bouncing off the hillside. 'You have one minute, man, and if by then you haven't answered we are coming in for you.'

Raleigh stood with his back against the rock face, knowing it was lies and there were no soldiers. Besides, if he had one minute, then there would be silence. But instead there was the sound of stealthy climbing. And escape through the fissure was closed to him. He withdrew from it and then, throwing his machete on to the flat where his hut had been, climbed swiftly down again. In the quick tropic vanishing of day it was now all but dark and he could see sudden stabbings of powerful torchlights on the foliage above the rock. Reaching the small flat area he scrabbled for and found his machete. He threw it accurately down the slope ahead of him, carefully following the twisting glitter of its sharpened edge; he could lose his sack, even his satchel, but the machete he had to have. Without it, the bush would be a foe instead of ally.

Now having carefully marked the area into which the cutlass has vanished, he took the satchel off his neck and threw it after the machete and even as he did so, he heard a voice above him. 'Raleigh you have just ten seconds.' And at once he was bathed in the light of a powerful torch held by someone evidently standing on a pinnacle of the rock behind him. He turned and the torchlight dazzled him. 'Stand quite still exactly as you are!' came a shouted order. 'We are coming down.'

Raleigh cursed, flung himself to the ground, stretched out his legs hard tight against each other, wriggled to the very edge of the dizzy slope, drew his arms up around his head, closed his eyes and rolled over it. The policemen on the pinnacle momentarily saw him go, a bundle rolling over and over like a log and gathering speed and then there was only the sound of him crashing down — then silence.

★　★　★

Joe Moseley was at home when Vair gave him the news. He was in his usual evening place on the front patio of his house on Stony Hill from which to view lower Kingston spread in a great arc below. It was a moonless night but the sky was a blaze of stars which seemed bent even to outdo the tremendous twinkling of the city's lights. He had his feet up on a chaise and a bottle of whisky close at hand. It was perhaps nine o'clock. The air was sweet with the scent of datura and night jasmine. A myriad of fireflies flickered. There were many regular and familiar sounds: the barking of distant dogs, the squeal of brakes and the hoot of cars, the croak of tree frogs, the raucous cry of a gecko, music floating up from somewhere down below, Marcia's instructing Thelma on some household matter. The heat of day was over. It was that perfect hour before bed summons those who will be astir by five-thirty in the morning. It was a time almost to match the joy of the first hours of a new Jamaican day before the sun dries out the dew. It was a time of day which if he could escape from functions, parties, meetings, Joe Moseley adored.

But tonight he was ill at ease. He had cancelled an evening appointment to be on hand for a call from Vair but none had come. When at last the telephone on the side table rang, he grabbed it fiercely.

'Moseley!'

'Joe . . . '

'Norman! What the devil you think you're

doing man leaving me all this time.'

'We've just got down. We don't have extensions in the John Crow mountains. You're the first person I've contacted.'

'Okay. You win. Sorry. Have you got him?'

'No. He got away.'

A wave of glee, totally improper in a Minister of Tourism who sees a major hotel project slipping from his grasp, seized Moseley and seized him unexpectedly. Through the long hours between now and Mason's departure he had been an unusually troubled man. His business was to promote tourism in Jamaica and on the whole it was an occupation he found satisfying. He was playing what was accepted as an important part in the country he loved — a part which allowed scope for travelling at the Government's expense and which brought him into contact with all manner of different people which, a gregarious man, on the whole he thoroughly enjoyed.

He had his doubts, being on occasions, as he had been that morning, uncertain whether offsetting the valuable foreign currency they brought against the social consequences of importing droves of sophisticated Americans and Canadians into the island was in the final analysis a worthwhile exercise; but he stilled his conscience by continually reminding himself that it was only the narrow fringe of land between the foothills of Jamaica's unbroken spine of mountains and the North Coast beaches which was sullied. The far, far greater part of his country was unchanged. There was the whole of the Southern Coast, there was Kingston, there were the inland townships and there was the huge mass of tree-girt hills and valleys which lay behind the first low ridge which were quite unknown to the vast majority of tourists and untrodden by them. Jamaica was, in effect, two countries and if it had been decided to sacrifice its smaller part for the benefit of the larger then as a loyal citizen he would make his contribution.

But in the afternoon meeting his doubts had been underlined. Whereas Mason had misread Moseley, Moseley had not misread Mason. He had seen him exactly for what he was. A crook. A man without scruples whose main purpose in life was in enriching himself and whose conscience would be untroubled whatever the consequences to others. And Lelia had been right to remind him about the Arawak Hotel. It had happened many years ago but it had been a catastrophe and many Jamaicans who had been persuaded to invest in it, including several of his own friends, and many local tradesmen, both large and small, who had been sub-contractors or suppliers of pottery and linen and the like had whistled for their money — some, even, had been bankrupted. And instinct — and Joe Moseley very much relied on instinct — instinct told him that in a project masterminded by Mason lay the seeds of another Arawak disaster.

Yet he was powerless to prevent it; his job was to carry out the Government's policy not design it. If Mason took up his option and raised the finance needed he would get his way. There would be objections by the rich people who had built their winter escape houses in San San and lip-service would be given to them but in the end planning approval would be given and the hotel would be built.

How strange it was. It was as if fate was playing a part. Here at the eleventh hour when a rogue was all but ready to put his signature to a document which Moseley's intuition insisted must result in grief for many, a murderer had intruded. And it was that murderer, and that murderer only, who offered deliverance. If Raleigh was caught, Mason would proceed; if he escaped he would not take up his option. Moseley was sure of that. It was after all not merely an option on a six acre piece of land and a shabby bungalow he would have to buy, but also Waterman's house, Petrea, costing as Mason himself had said about two million dollars. And that, until he resold it, would be Mason's personal investment. And as he had pointed out — without actually saying so in as many words — with a murderer armed with a loaded revolver at large the value of San San property must fall.

In the long run Raleigh would be caught. It could take weeks, even possibly months to achieve but in fact all that was needed was a breathing-space. Twenty-four hours would do. And here was Norman Vair offering it to him.

There was just one question. He controlled himself to put it in the way it should be put by a Jamaican with his country's interests at heart.

'Man!' he cried. 'What you saying? Got away. How could he have got away? You told me yourself this morning you had got his way out covered.'

'He got away,' said Vair quietly. 'He lay down and rolled away from us. Just like that. It was quite remarkable. He rolled like a log and he didn't stop rolling until the bushes stopped him rolling any more.'

Moseley thought of the proverb he had quoted to Lelia: *When rock starts tumble down hill, him not stop until him reach bottom.* It was weird — as if all had been foreseen.

He asked the question: 'So he's got away. Gun and all?'

'No,' said Vair, 'we've got the gun.'

And he explained. How Raleigh had pitched first his sack and then his satchel ahead of him. And while his sack had been reclaimable, the strap of the satchel had caught on a high branch of one of the trees growing from the bottom of the slope and in the satchel had been Bannister's gun!

'So, you can go to bed happy now?' said Vair.

'No, man!' said Moseley.

'Joe, we'll catch him,' Vair said reassuringly. 'It may take a few days, but we'll catch him this time. And anyway until we do the situation isn't, apart from poor old Bannister, so very different from how it was yesterday, is it, Joe?'

And that was the trouble. That it wasn't. And when Mason discovered, when San San discovered, that it wasn't different, Mason would take up his option.

But if . . .

'Norman,' Moseley said, 'who have you told about the gun being found?'

'Joe. I'm phoning from Fairy Hill Post

Office. We've just got down. I've got a bunch of policemen who're bloody tired and hungry and scratched to ribbons waiting in a van to leave for Port Antonio . . . '

'So no one else knows? That you've got the gun?'

'Only the men who were with me?'

'Norman, I want you to do something for me and not ask why.'

For once Vair sounded impatient: 'What, Joe?'

'I want you to make sure your men don't tell anyone you've found that gun for twenty-four hours. And that you don't tell anyone else yourself. Will you do that for me, Norman?'

'You mean not report it. Not even to Huie? Jeeze, man . . . '

'Norman, I beg of you.'

'You asking me to suppress a piece of information that is vital for the . . . '

'Not suppress it, Norman.' And Joe Moseley chuckled, knowing he would have his way. 'Just keep it sub rosa for a day.'

Night Flight

'Only birds and fools fly —
and birds don't fly at night'.
(Old R.A.F. saying)

1

'I don't know how you find your way.'

'You get used to it,' she said.

'Even on a pitch-black night like this?'

'You get used to it.'

He knew what she was trying to convey: Look, leading aircraftsman Mitchell, it's what I do — ferry adolescents like you around Montrose airfield. It's what I do and that's the beginning and the end of it so far as you're concerned. And you'll be wasting your time trying to use it as an opening gambit if that's what you've got in mind.

It wasn't what he had in mind — it was just that he couldn't endure the silence between them. Silence left you free to think. Free to imagine what might lie ahead. To remember what lay in the immediate past, remember a thud, dull but loud enough to have you pause in the act of playing a card, loud enough to have had the others look at you as if somehow you had been responsible for it; a thud so clear in its meaning that when you threw open the door and stared out into the night, the sickening yellow ball of flame on the sand dune to the north came as no surprise.

'I'm not trying to pick you up, Miss Rivers,' he said.

'Corporal Rivers.'

'Yes. Well I'm not. That would be silly wouldn't it?'

She did not reply but his uneasiness forced him to go on talking.

'I mean you're different aren't you? I mean you ought to be an officer.'

'What an extraordinary thing to say.' She still didn't turn her head but the set of it and the fineness of her profile seen in the faint glow thrown by the dashboard instruments seemed to confirm what he was saying.

'No, it's not,' he insisted obstinately. 'You're not like any of the other Waafs. You don't walk like they do. You don't talk like they do. You don't even sit like they do when you're driving a Commer.' And if he hadn't lacked the courage he might have added: 'I bet no one's ever taken *you* on Montrose beach and tried undoing *your* tunic buttons!'

'You know, you really are a stupid boy,' she said. 'And it's very embarrassing. So please be quiet.'

And he was — until they got to the far end of the airfield where she hauled the Commer bumpily round so that it was headed towards the sea, then put the gears into neutral because there was a Master in the circuit.

They could follow its course by its navigation lights as it progressed a thousand feet up along the down-wind leg. But the night was so dark that all they could see of it were the red and green navigation lights on its wingtips and the white light at the tail, the flames from its exhausts and a faint glow from the cockpit. The sight of the Master magnified his fear and forced him to talk about it.

'I'm sorry if what I said upset you,' he told her, 'but that was a friend of mine who bought it half an hour ago. Pete Garland. We shared a billet.'

'I know. I've collected you both before.' Her tone stayed factual, without a hint of sympathy. But after a moment she added, with a little warmth: 'You mustn't let it worry you. You'll be all right. Like he will be.' She nodded her head towards the Master that was past them now and starting its crosswind turn.

'How long have you been doing this?' he asked. 'I mean ferrying pupils?'

'About six courses.'

He wondered how many she'd ferried over and not brought back.

'I wouldn't,' he complained, 'have been flying tonight if Garland hadn't bought it. It's a bit thick, isn't it, hauling out the fellow who shares a man's billet just because he's killed himself and made room for someone else to have a go at doing the same bloody thing?'

'They've got to get through the course and I suppose yours was the next name on the list.'

'Yes,' he said, 'you're quite right. I've no business making you a shoulder to cry on. But it was one hell of a shock. He was a very good friend of mine. I was playing cards . . . and we heard it . . . and . . . Well I don't mind admitting it, we're all a bit frightened of night flying, anyway. I bet even Wilson is although he'd never admit to it.'

'Why Wilson in particular?'

'You know who I mean?'

'The boy with ginger hair.'

'Yes. I have to do under the hood with him.'

She understood. One of the exercises a would-be pilot had to practice was flying blind on instruments. He pulled a hood up over him and a co-pupil occupied the forward cockpit to guard against accidents. But the more harum-scarum pupils seized the only opportunity they got for showing off in front of another member of the course and not infrequently killed themselves.

'Some of you are such bloody fools,' she said. 'Why don't you just put your foot down and say no?'

'It's difficult.'

She could understand that too; there were different kinds of courage. She wondered how Freddie had coped with it. He'd never talked about it. Had hardly talked flying at all for all that, apart from her, flying had been his life. Married to an R. A. F. Cranwell-trained career officer now locked away in a Stalag Luft she'd had to become a Waaf to gain her first real inkling of what was involved. Now, after several months at Montrose, she knew in considerable detail what the trainee pilots did; including what they did on their illegal low-flying jaunts and what a terrifying business it could be for the passenger putting up with it scared-stiff but having to make out he'd enjoyed it when they landed. But the fear of the boy beside her now, a boy who'd been brought over to take the place of another who'd just killed himself, was of a deeper dimension, a fear which came like a wave, almost tangible, filling the cab. He was, she guessed, even more frightened now than he was when enduring Wilson doing his split-arse turns at nearly zero feet with the Master juddering on the margin of an incipient spin and certain death guaranteed for both of them by the least misjudgement. She understood why — until they'd got enough experience there was something nerve-wracking about night flying which the other for all its danger lacked.

'There's as many killed low flying at Montrose as there are night flying,' she pointed out.

'That right? I mean . . . ' He hesitated. 'I mean it's gone on the same with all the courses you've been ferrying? Average of five killed in every course? About ten per cent?'

'I don't think we should be talking this way. All your concentration should be on what you've got to do not on what can happen if you do it wrongly. After all you're not being asked to do anything that's very difficult.'

'It's the flaps,' he said. 'If they make you go round again. That's what gets most of them. They end up in the Basin. Not that it could have been that with poor old Pete . . . Garland. What happened to him's a mystery.'

He turned his head sideways to stare at the Master now turning in to make its final approach wondering which one of the course was flying it. Just about now, he thought, he'll see the hooded glim lamps that aren't visible from a higher altitude and he'll pick up the glide path indicator and the colour he sees will tell him if he was too flat or too steep or just right and in a minute he'll switch on his landing lights and if it all goes well he'll bump it down and say thank God that one's over.

But if he messes it up and gets a red and has to go round again that's when it'll be dangerous. Because of those bloody flaps!

'Well,' he heard her saying through his thoughts, 'remember if you have to go round again exactly what you've got to do. Look. Why not go through it with me now? What you do if they give you a red.' And when he didn't respond. 'Go on! Say it!'

He still hesitated, then brought it out in a rush: 'Open throttle to maximum power. Retract undercarriage a.s.a.p. Climb to at least four hundred feet and be doing a hundred miles an hour before starting to get the flaps up. And get them up slowly adjusting the trimming all the time.' He could have been reading from the manual.

'Well that doesn't sound very difficult does it?'

'No,' he admitted. 'It doesn't sound difficult . . . But we've already lost Barker and Dacre doing it. And now . . . '

He broke off as the beams of the approaching Master's landing lights suddenly, startlingly, pierced the blackness and the steadily increasing engine note killed the night's silence. They watched the machine all the way down, their heads turning slowly. When it hit the runway it bounced alarmingly high, and their pulses raced, but it bounced again, less this time, and settled on the grass and after a while Mitchell couldn't see it for Julie River's head and shoulders. And then it was in view again, taxying towards the dispersal hut.

'There you are,' she said. 'A piece of cake.'

She made to drop the gear lever in but Mitchell stopped her. He had the feeling that the longer he could delay getting to the dispersal hut the greater his chances of surviving the night would be.

'There can't be all that hurry,' he said. 'Let's chat for a bit.' He put his hand on her arm. 'Please.'

She threw it off. Irritably. 'Don't do that!'

Something one of the other Waafs had said in the pub to Fox who was in number nineteen course as well, came to him: 'If you want to get anywhere with Corporal Rivers, Charlie, you'd better buy yourself a kilt.' He'd got the drift of that but not really understood — his sexual knowledge was minimal, his sexual experience limited to once fondling a breast still covered by a bra. In a way he was envious of those who hinted boldly with broad winks about their exploits with the Montrose Waafs. But in fact Waafs didn't interest him. There was something about the coarse texture of their stockings, the flatness of their shoes, the masculinity of their dress,

218

that seemed the absolute antithesis of femininity. At the Angus Dance Hall it was only the civilian girls he asked to dance with him. And afterwards he would lie on his metal bed recalling the delicious excitement of a thigh against his own, of firm soft breasts against his chest and imagine the girl who had attracted him most of all that evening slowly undress, remembering in astonishing detail the blouse and skirt or the dress she'd worn. But he'd always give her silk stockings to unroll slowly one by one, or allow him to unroll, and lacy underwear. And he never had her strip quite naked because there had to be some mystery left. Without mystery a girl was less than perfect.

'I'm sorry,' he said. 'It didn't mean anything. I mean, I don't think of you that way . . . ' He broke off miserably, appalled by his own gaucheness.

She laughed, not harshly, but as as if she was laughing at herself.

'How do you think of me then?' she said. And when he didn't reply. 'Go on, I want to know.'

There was something so totally superior about her, in her beauty (because she was very beautiful); in her experience (because she could give him six or seven years); in her quality (for she was clearly of a higher class);

and above all in what he took to be her total self-assurance, that he found it impossible not to answer, and answer honestly.

'Well, I don't quite know how to put it. I mean, I know it's going to sound rude, but . . . well you could be an aunt . . . ', and, hastily, 'if I had a young one, I mean. Or an older sister.'

'An aunt or an older sister.' There was the same self-deprecatory chuckle. 'How old do you think I am? Forty? I'm twenty-six.'

'Yes, well that's about what I thought. What most of us reckon . . . '

'Go on. Don't hold back.' She had turned in the cab and was resting her back against the door to it, studying him as best she could in the dashboard glow. 'So you talk about me.'

'Well, you're very pretty and . . . well, different. And the Waafs talk a lot about you, when we're with them.'

And none it very complimentary, she mused. But that was an unimportant thought. What was more interesting was why, for the first time since she'd put on uniform, she'd allowed herself to be drawn into a conversation *about* herself. And with an artless youth who'd probably only just rid himself of pimples. She leaned forward to switch off the engine and noticed his instinctive flinching.

'What's your first name?' she demanded.

'Harry.'

'And you're what? Nineteen? Twenty?'

'Twenty.'

'What did you do before you joined up?'

'Nothing much. Just school and . . . And I had a job for a bit. Not much of a job.'

She didn't press him. 'Which you gave up to become a pilot?'

'Yes.'

'Why?'

'Why?' It seemed a strange question.

'Yes, why?'

'Well I'd have been called up anyway.'

'You're not answering my question. You could have volunteered to drive a tank. Or joined the Navy. Or if you *had* to go into the Raf, got yourself a nice safe groundstaff job. So why volunteer to be a pilot and risk what's happened to Garland and Dacre and the other one, happening to you?'

'It's just something I wanted to do.' He spoke almost sulkily.

'You wanted to do suddenly? Or over a long time?'

He thought about it. It was funny but he didn't quite know how to answer her. 'Well it sort of grew, I think,' he said eventually.

'Have you,' she said, 'got a girl friend? . . . Back home I mean.'

He shook his head. 'No, not really. Well there's one or two . . . but no, not really.'

'Did you think that being a pilot would help you get yourself a girl friend? Was that it?'

He would have denied it to anyone else but he couldn't with her. 'Well, I suppose . . . I suppose that was part of it.'

Part, she thought, just part. But probably an important part. How different he was, this boy, from Freddie. Freddie secure in his background, in his charm, his flair, his rank, his certainty. And yet supposing this boy did get his wings, as most probably he would, not having been ploughed this far, and possessed a natural ability for flying as maybe he had — an ability to fly was after all no more related to background and education than was being able to drive a Commer! Well he'd only get sergeant's stripes to start with but if the war went on long enough and he survived long enough then sooner or later he'd be commissioned. And give him a year or two in an officer's uniform, with a brevet on his chest and a gong or two below it and you wouldn't recognize him. And that was what it was all about, why he wanted to be a pilot, not because he was wild on flying as Freddie had been almost since he got out of rompers but because for all his artlessness, there was in Harry Mitchell an urge to better himself, to lift himself out of the rut of insignificance. Clumsy he might be, gauche, unworldly, but there was in the boy that essential spark without which progress was impossible; and enough romance to have chosen this of all ways.

She could imagine him amongst his fellow pupils, quiet, withdrawn, never a leading light. Yes, of course it would be impossible for him to resist risking his neck at Wilson's whim. In the Saloon Bar of the Crown which was the favourite Montrose pub amongst the trainee pilots, Wilson would be a leading light, shooting his lines, cracking his jokes, holding his own with ease. Harry — she thought of him now as Harry which was odd — Harry would be hovering somewhere, eager to buy his round, happy enough just to be accepted. And when it came to girls? He'd probably be messy. Even furtive. Possibly the stuff of which cinema pests were made, men who changed their seats two or three times through a performance and shifted their knee against your own in the vain hope you'd respond. Not because they were necessarily over-sexed but because they were desperate for feminine contact but hadn't the style or had so little confidence in themselves. But, with the right trappings to set you off, style could be cultivated; and self-confidence in sex required only a few successful experiences. If anyone knew that, God knows it should be her.

'They're important to you, aren't they?' she hazarded. 'Girls?'

'Yes,' he muttered, feeling the burning of his cheeks, grateful for the gloominess of the cab, the pitch-blackness of the night.

'There's a lot of pretty Waafs on the station.' She couldn't resist it and anyway perhaps it helped him: 'I mean amongst the kind you wouldn't think of as aunts or sisters?'

'S'pose so.'

'You don't think so?' She was genuinely surprised.

'No. Not really.'

'Oh.' She was puzzled.

'They all seem . . . well, sort of crude.'

'Well some of them are, of course. But only some.'

'I don't mean it that way. But I can't explain it.'

Won't, you mean, she thought, reading his tone. 'Do you find me crude?' she said.

'No, of course not.'

'Why of course not?'

'I told you. You're different. You ought to be an officer.' And boldly: 'Why aren't you?'

'Because I chose not to be.'

He didn't disbelieve her for a moment. 'Why?' he asked.

'I had my reasons. Reasons much too complicated to explain to you.'

★　★　★

It had come full circle. For a space she had allowed herself to have become involved even touched the edge of intimacy but his questioning was a reminder of the very reasons why she had chosen the path she had. A reminder of how careful she had to be all the time through the years and years which had to be got through before the war was over and she and Freddie were reunited.

Abruptly she switched the ignition on.

'There's another Master taxying out,' she said. 'I can get you over before it gets here.'

'I've said something that upsets you, haven't I?' he said.

'You haven't upset me in the least,' she answered coldly.

But at the dispersal hut she broke a resolution by touching him on the arm as he was about to go.

'Good luck, Harry,' she said. 'I'll come and collect you when it's over.'

2

'Shut the fucking door!'

He did so regretfully, abandoning the faint hope there'd be a parting wave that others might see. He stood for a moment looking around the hut, trying to establish who else of nineteen course was there and recognized three. Some of the rest he knew by sight but not by name: they were of eighteen course, the last batch of eighteen still to do their first solo night flights.

'You're Mitchell?'

He turned towards the duty officer who sat behind the only piece of furniture, an old kitchen table with a telephone on it.

'Yes, Sir.'

'Okay.' The duty officer did something with a pencil. 'Find yourself a pew and try and get a bit of sleep. You're not going to be wanted for quite a while.'

He looked round the hut. Well it wasn't really a hut, more an overblown packing case with a door at one end of it. There wasn't a window — a window would have presented an extra blackout problem — and the air was hazed with tobacco smoke which smarted his eyes abominably. There were so many pupils in flying kit sprawled about, sitting in small groups chatting or, the lucky ones who'd got there early, lying down using their parachutes as pillows, that at first he could nowhere see an empty space. When eventually he found one, lumbered with his parachute and impeded by his still stiff flying boots, it wasn't easy stepping over recumbent bodies to get to it. 'Looks like a bloody battlefield, doesn't it? Join the Raf and find yourself in Calcutta!' was the only sympathy he got and this from someone he didn't know. The point eluded him so he agreed it did and busied himself extracting with considerable difficulty his cigarette case out of an inner pocket. He was contemplating the wisdom of offering one to the pupil who'd spoken to him when the telephone abruptly rang. The effect was remarkable. Conversation ceased and except for heads turning towards the duty officer, the hut was of a sudden filled with statues, upraised hands held motionless cigarettes, a man shifting his position to be more comfortable remained bent over, stiff as a ramrod, knee on floor.

The duty officer answered crisply: 'Right!' put the phone back on the hook and glancing at his list called: 'Freeman!' From out of the welter of bodies one extracted itself and with great difficulty, encumbered by gear staggered rather than stepped over those between him and the door, placing his feet carefully in such spaces as he could find for them. At the door where there was more room because it was the coldest place he put on his helmet, fixed his goggles, slid his hands into silk undergloves, woollen gloves and gauntlets, lifted the parachute he'd allowed to slip to the floor and with it swinging clumsily behind him blundered out. One or two 'good lucks' drifted after him into the night.

★ ★ ★

Mitchell lit his cigarette, put the case away and secretly started counting. He made it seventeen including himself. It ought to be thirteen times twenty minutes, four hours and twenty minutes before they'd started on course nineteen. But obviously it wasn't working that way or Garland wouldn't have been sent out. And Garland wouldn't have killed himself. And he wouldn't be sitting here sweating on it now. What the hell were they up to, sending nineteen course pupils out ahead of eighteen's? Maybe there'd been a reason. Maybe Garland had volunteered or something?

* * *

The snarl of an engine cut across his thoughts and stifled such desultory conversation as had restarted. Thin blue threads of smoke climbed straight to the blackened ceiling. Only the duty officer was pretending not to listen, scrawling something in his notebook. The engine note became a roar and the hut shivered a trifle from its vibration. The sound began to fade into a hum and as it did conversation restarted, louder than before, more forced. Why don't we just say it, Mitchell thought? Why don't we shout it out? 'Freeman's unstuck, lucky bugger! Now all he's got to do is get the bloody thing down again!'

* * *

An hour and more passed. Freeman had done his three circuits and landings. So had Wakeman and Glyn-Davies. There was no sense to it. It wasn't even alphabetical. But at least there was enough room now to lie stretched out using the parachute pack as pillow. They were hard and the curve of them held your head up in an unnatural angle. So they weren't very comfortable; but they were comforting. To his surprise he was feeling drowsy. But it was warm in the hut, the double blackout door kept the winter out. You would never have known there was still patches of snow outside and the Grampians were covered. It had been a hard winter. For a time the airfield had been deep in snow and the Commanding Officer had conceived the brilliant idea of having the entire station's complement, every man-jack of it, lined up at one end of the airfield and then he had led the way two paces ahead, his great-coat flapping in the bitter wind, like a Russian general leading the Reds, or maybe the Whites, in a march across the steppes against the enemy. He'd looked impressive the C. O., swashbuckling, leading the long straggling line of hundreds and hundreds of men and women in Air Force blue marching through the snow. It had been like something in a film. But when they got to the end and turned round to see what they had done it had been a let-down. Almost funny! For instead of the snow being flattened enough for them to restart flying, there was nothing but a few footprints in it!

Well, thank God, most of the snow at the lower levels had melted in that brief milder spell but the wind was from the north-east again and outside it was cold enough to freeze the balls off a brass monkey. You had to search for places to be really warm. Like this one was! Or had been — when the hut had been packed to bursting. It was colder now. By the time it was his turn to fly it'd probably be freezing. But it'd still be warm in the aircrew mess. The lucky buggers who were fireproof because they'd done their night solos on moonlit nights 'd be sitting round playing brag and solo without a care in the whole darn world. And long before he'd got to do his solo they'd have packed it in and gone off to their billets. Inevitably his thoughts shifted to his own billet which had been one of the warmest, the cosiest of all. They'd been lucky, he and Pete Garland. Instead of an iron bed in a hut with a double row of beds which was what most of the course had to accept they'd been allocated the end room of a hut which had two iron beds in it and a stove of its own and what they'd got into doing was banking the stove up high and leaving its door open so that when they were nice and snug under the blankets they could watch the firelight flickering on the walls while they listened to *Stardust* played endlessly on Pete's portable. And then when sleep started taking over, Pete, who had been imaginative, and had fixed up a complicated arrangement of strings, would pull on one of them and it would shut the fire door. Well it was there to go back to, the stove, and Pete's portable . . .

'Tremlett!'

As another pupil got to his feet Mitchell fell to wondering just how many the duty officer had sent to their deaths. To date, including Garland, three had been killed in nineteen course — all night flying. And not half the course gone solo. Well what could you expect? An airfield strung between an icy sea on one side and mountains on the other. With sand dunes you had to clear one end in landing and the bloody great Montrose Basin to catch you if you messed it up on take-off. And a bastard of an aircraft like the Master. It was criminal, that's what it was, bloody criminal. They ought to reserve night flying to moonlit nights. No one pranged on them. And no one . . .

'Mitchell!'

He couldn't believe his ears.

'Mitchell!' The duty officer's voice was testy.

'Yes, Sir?' he asked.

'Well get to your feet, man. We haven't got all night.'

He couldn't credit it. What about . . . ? He couldn't remember the name of the pupil who'd been called before him and who was making his way back to the place he'd quitted moments earlier.

'I'm nineteen course, Sir,' he called out desperately.

'I know what course you're on, Mitchell. I've got it written down here. Now jump to.'

* * *

He struggled to his feet, his body stiff, a crick somewhere in his neck. As he searched in the gloom for his helmet and the rest of it, his eyes filled with tears of anger, fear, frustration. It wasn't fair. It just wasn't bloody fair! Why pick on him? Why not at least give him a fair crack of the whip? Quite often when the weather closed in they had to pack it in early and then with any luck the next call didn't come until the moon had started coming up. As likely as not that's what would happen tonight — after he'd killed himself! He was quite sure he was going to kill himself. He was gripped by a terrible panic like that of a man crossing a narrow walkway with a precipice both sides suddenly struck blind; or of a man who has forgotten all he has been taught and now has to face a crisis for which he is totally unprepared. 'Feel, okay, Mitchell?' his instructor (who was in fact tonight's duty officer) had said. 'Ready for me to put you down for solo?' What could you say but 'Yes, Sir'? And it had seemed all right. Five circuits and bumps they'd done and Shipman had been pleased with him. You could tell it in his voice. He'd been wishing him into agreeing he was ready. You couldn't say no. But that had been Tuesday. That was three nights ago. That had been before Pete Garland killed himself . . .

3

'Good luck.' The words stayed with him in the dark outside. From the north the wind moaned through the sand dunes knifing his cheeks and after the comparative brightness of the dispersal hut the darkness of the night was absolute. Ungainly with the parachute bouncing against his rump he stumbled out across the grass to the waiting Master guided by the blue pencil light of a torch held by an invisible member of the groundstaff. Willing hands helped him up and in. He felt the warmth of a close human body. He would have spoken but he could think of nothing to say. 'Good luck,' again. Did they always say that, he wondered? Or was it because of Garland?

★ ★ ★

Pulled tight, the straps over thighs and shoulders were comforting. He slid the cockpit cover shut only at once to see to his horror, directly above, about to land on top of him, another aircraft, it's green and red navigation lights mere inches above his head!

Panic-stricken he slammed the Perspex cockpit cover open again for all that it was far too late to get out in time . . . and the aircraft vanished. Sick with relief, he laughed at his own idiocy, an odd choking laugh that was more a sob; for the lights had been his own wingtip lights reflected in the canopy.

★   ★   ★

Having taxied to the end of the airfield he waited for the green of an Aldis lamp to signal approval for take-off. Ahead of him was a faint line of lights, meanly lit and meanly spaced. These were the well-named glim lamps, low-powered and covered with small hoods so as to be visible only from low altitudes. Apart from them and the cheerful colours of the cockpit lamps there was only blackness. Around him lay the mystery of the airfield. To his left the invisible sea surging steadily against the sandy beach, to his right the wartime station without so much as a glow to advertise its presence to the enemy and beyond it a narrowish stretch of more or less level land before the Grampians, rising steeply to a height of several thousand feet, began. Behind him were the sand dunes as much as a hundred and fifty feet in height into which only an hour or two before for some unaccountable reason Garland had crashed in making his first and only solo night approach; ahead, at the end of the airfield, lay the Montrose Basin, approaching two miles square, a curious stretch of water connected to the ocean by a slender channel into which too many aircraft had crashed through pilot error. Above was the limitless night.

But he was more secure now. Dual and solo he had flown more than eighty hours in Masters, and a hundred and twenty in aircraft altogether, and the familiar feeling of the controls while taxying out had reassured him. As, unknown to him, Julie Rivers, had surmised, he was an able pilot, born with an instinctive sense of balance and the degree of caution essential for longevity. He might lack the dash and flair of a Wilson but in the end was likely to prove a more useful member of a squadron. Still extremely nervous of what lay ahead he was, nevertheless, able to contemplate with wistful envy the hundreds of men and women who in invisible control tower, messes, billets, were going about their business without fear of what the next twenty minutes or so might bring; but it was not without a little pride that he reflected that for those twenty minutes what he was doing was what the airfield was all about. That in effect, a thousand and more men and women, were only there at all because of him.

* * *

The signal stabbed the darkness underlining the point: his was the airfield, his the station's operation. He made the final essential checks: that the mixture control was set to normal rich, the airscrew in fine pitch, the undercarriage and flap levers fully neutral, the various temperatures as they should be, the radiator shutter open, the trim tabs correct.

He opened the throttle gently pushing it forward to its fullest extent, very conscious of the roundness of its ball against his palm and he eased the control column forward sufficiently for the tail to be a little below flying position. As the aircraft gathered speed, bumping across the uneven ground, he adjusted the slight tendency to swing away from the meagre line of glim lamps by a touch of rudder. And then, it seemed simultaneously, the bumping ceased and the glim lamps vanished. He was airborne. At once he retraced the undercarriage and from practice born of experience let his hand slip off the throttle on to the large elevator trimming wheel to counteract the feeling of tail heaviness. He noted with satisfaction the lights of the undercarriage position indicator change from green to red; the wheels were safely locked away. Returning his hand to the throttle lever he shifted his gaze to the vital central instrument panel which told him the essential things: his airspeed, altitude, rate of climb, his turn and bank, his directional heading and, and this most important of all, the relationship of the Master to the invisible horizon. The world outside for the moment did not exist. As Julie Rivers had said in this first stage at least what he had to do was simple: keep the aircraft climbing steadily and levelly until he reached one thousand feet.

Eyes glued to these instruments, correcting the least flaw in what they advised him with the care and precision of a surgeon conducting the most delicate of operations, his confidence mounted steadily. What he was doing, he reassured himself, was exactly what he had done with distinction in Link Trainer exercises. A dozen times cocooned in that strange toy he had taken off and landed an aircraft safely; even better, by picking up different signals he had, theoretically lost in cloud, homed in on radio beacons and put down successfully in thick fog on new and nameless airfields. And a Link Trainer, he reminded himself, was a far more sensitive creature than a Miles Master.

At one thousand feet he executed a rate-one ninety degree turn crosswind. The Montrose Basin, he reflected, would be directly beneath him now, Dacre and Barker's graveyard, and the graveyard of others in many earlier courses. But the thought failed to bring the expected shaft of fear and for the first time he permitted a glance away from his instruments with the vague idea of perhaps seeing the glimmer of water below. But there was nothing to see, nothing but the red and green wingtip lights and blue and yellow flames flickering like marsh gas along the fuselage from the exhausts.

Judging the correct time to make his second turn he brought the Master back along the reciprocal course of take-off on the downwind leg. He would be fairly well out now over the sea, he reflected, the winter-cold grey North Sea — and he imagined the breakers dying on the beach and he thought about the Scottish girl he had picked up in the dance hall and how they had lain together there, for all that it was very cold, kissing and cuddling but nothing more. It was only a flash of a thought as was also a sudden image, come and gone as quickly, of Corporal Rivers in the Commer. And then it was time to lower the undercarriage. He throttled back a little, and then rather more, his eyes glued to his airspeed indicator and then, when his speed had dropped to less than a hundred and fifty miles an hour, he reached for the undercarriage lever downside to his left and firmly lowered it. With a sense of infinite satisfaction he felt the crunch of the wheels locking down and saw the red lights vanish from the panel and green lights take their place.

There were only two more turns to make. The turn crosswind when he must reduce speed further to less than a hundred and thirty miles an hour before lowering the dreaded flaps and then the turn into wind for landing. He made the first meticulously and lowering the flaps compensated for the excess load on the control column as the nose began dropping down by an adjustment of the trimming tabs. I must remember, he told himself, not to allow my speed to drop below eighty miles an hour and especially in that final turn I must keep the nose up with top rudder. He said these things aloud. It was all bookwork stuff. He was an efficient youngster cocooned in a tiny cockpit trained to accept that so long as he stuck strictly to what the manual and the instructors had told him, there would be no problems.

He made the final turn. A degree of nervousness, for the past few minutes entirely lost in the effort of total concentration, returned. If his timing had been correct he would be heading for the centre of the airfield; if incorrect too much perhaps to one side or the other. But it was broad; there was margin for a reasonable error. Making an engine-assisted approach he started losing height, his eyes darting up from the main instrument panel through the cockpit hood for the first sight of the glide path indicator, then down again to check aircraft altitude and speed. He was talking continually, encouragingly to himself. 'Don't think,' he said, 'you're going to see those glim lamps until you get well down because you won't. Just keep it steady, Harry Mitchell, keep it steady.' He was tense but confident, certain he'd made a good job of things. Any moment now . . . yes, there it was! The glide path indicator! Amber! Too high! Should he throttle back or increase the line of attack? He glanced quickly at the airspeed indicator. Eighty-four miles an hour! Not over-much margin there! He pushed the nose down slightly and after moments which seemed to pass with excruciating slowness the amber light abruptly vanished to be replaced by green. It was a question of fine judgement now. He mustn't get too fast, mustn't dive too steeply. Yes, the thing to do now that he'd got the green was ease back on the stick to hold it there. Ease back a trifle, not too much to cause the speed to fall too low but the moment the amber came back again ease forward.

★　★　★

'Ah!' He let out a cry of exultation as the line of glim lamps magically materialized proving his circuit had been one of impressive accuracy and with an overpowering sense of glee reached for and pulled on the landing lamps lever but even as the two brilliant beams streamed out raking the night, proving the solid human world existed, a contrary light flashed at him from the invisible control tower. Red for danger! But it said more, far more than that! It said GO ROUND AGAIN! He stared at it horror-stricken. 'Why?' he shouted. 'Why? Why? Why?' The light kept winking, winking red. DO AS YOU'RE TOLD. GO ROUND AGAIN! It did not occur to him to disobey. There had to be a reason. Another aircraft in the circuit maybe? Some obstacle on the ground? He refused to believe the error could be his own.

In utter chagrin he opened the throttle and pulled the control column back and at once his rising wingtips hid the flashing Aldis lamp and the brilliant rays of his landing lamps streamed upwards losing themselves in the inky void above. The Master until then delightfully smooth and responsive became a lumbering tank, fighting the braking effect of lowered flaps and wheels. Seizing the undercarriage lever he rammed it upwards. The reassuring green lights vanished as he pressured against the control column to equate the change of trim. He felt the wheels lock up, saw the red lights flash on. He felt the drip of sweat run down his sides. Now came the danger time. You had to raise the flaps — but raise them too quickly and the nose will rear and flick you into an incipient spin, corkscrewing you down into Montrose Basin. As had happened to Barker. And Dacre. And many more. Everything but the thought of flaps was obliterated from his mind. The landing lamps streamed on, forgotten. He must raise them slowly, fraction by fraction. As he raised them the nose would tend to rise; he must compensate by forward pressure on the stick and with the other hand feel for the trimming wheel and wind it forward. Gingerly he reached down for the flap lever, a lever smaller than the undercarriage lever but located very near to it, and raised it slightly. The effect was immediate, the aircraft seeming to weigh back against the control column against which his right hand pushed. He slipped his left hand to the trimming wheel and wound it slightly forward. At once the pressure eased. He moved his hand back to the flap lever and raised it a trifle more, pressed against the control column, adjusted the trim. And so continued until at last it had been achieved, the flaps were fully raised.

It was only then he realised he was soaked in sweat; his body in its sidcot, uniform and underclothes, his hands within three layers of gloves, his head inside the helmet. But he had done it. Succeeded where Dacre and Barker had failed. Where others had failed. Weak with relief he relaxed and it was then he saw the beams from his landing lamps raking the night and he swore and hastily switched them off. But how far, he wondered, had he flown? In the relief he was still alive this did not at first strike him as important but as an interesting question. Had he cleared the Basin? Yes, presumably — it was less than two miles wide. And after the Basin, what? There wasn't a problem, was there? There weren't any hills? No, the Grampians were to the right. He turned his head as if to look through the Perspex for them and to his horror saw two eyes glaring back at him. The immediate effect was as chilling as to a woman who hearing a noise draws back night-curtains to see a face staring in. It took moments for him to realise that the ebony night made blacker by the glow within the cockpit turned the cockpit hood into a mirror. That it was useless looking out, that the night was utterly impenetrable. Then the mountains for all he knew could be ahead of him! The throttle was still wide open, he'd forgotten all about it, forgotten the engine noise, forgotten everything except the flaps! Forgotten to check his heading!

Immediately an utter certainty that he was heading directly for the Grampians seized him and at once he hauled the Master round to port and held it there putting distance between him and the imagined mountains. But then he thought if I go too far out to sea, I shall lose the land. And he did not know what to do. He began peering, wildly, looking in all directions. And saw nothing. Only blackness. And his own frightened, staring eyes. With sudden surprise he realised the seriousness of his predicament. Without radio contact — for the Masters at No. 8 R.A.F. Flying School, Montrose, were not equipped with radio — without radio contact he was lost in a pitch black night, all sense of direction gone, with somewhere the sea, somewhere the mountains and God alone knew where, the airfield!

And now he knew something which was even worse than fear: a sense of devastating loneliness. And blindness — as if sight was limited by the confines of his cockpit.

Panic is a pilot's greatest danger. His security, his hope of returning to the land of living men and women, is utterly dependant on his ability to integrate precise and delicate movements with his hands and feet with the instructions issued by a cool, clear, thinking mind. But panic can utterly destroy the relationship of mind and body, so that the one can be concerned with horrible imaginings while the other thrashes wildly spurred by instincts which do not necessarily have validity. Moreover, normally the mind has many aids such as sight and memory which are wanting in total darkness. Night, of course, is never entirely black. Even if there is no moon and a layer of cloud shuts out the stars, the eyes, albeit gradually, adjust so that it may be possible by the application of grim determination and utter concentration eventually just to pick out a faint horizon and use that as a guide. But to achieve this from an aircraft it is essential to destroy such light as you have about you, and specifically your cockpit and your navigation lights. This, with his lack of experience and in the terrible stress of the moment, Mitchell did not think of doing. On the contrary the greens and reds and whites and ambers of the various instruments were a source of comfort, the only proof that he had sight and that a tangible world outside the Master did exist; voluntarily to plunge himself into inky blackness, to, as it were, draw the horrid night into the cockpit itself, even had he thought of doing so, would have been an unimaginable proposition. And so looking this way and that — up, down, sideways — rewarded only by his own desperate face staring back at him, he began to lose control, paying less and less attention to his instruments, to what his hands and feet were doing, driven by the absurd conviction that only his eyes could save him.

It was the sound which rescued him. At first he heard it as no more than a gentle hiss, a weird distraction from the important things on hand. And then it was something more: a feeling of *resistance*. Momentarily abandoning his hopeless peering into vacuum and glancing at the instrument panel he noticed that his speed had crept higher than it should while his altimeter told him he was losing height. He found this intensely irritating. He needed all his faculties to spot some pinprick somewhere which would tell him at least if he was over land or sea. He hauled back roughly on the control column to raise the Master's nose and recommenced with steadily mounting desperation his search through the cockpit's Perspex. But the sound insisted; indeed increased. Glaring angrily at the instruments he saw to his amazement that his speed was even faster and that not only was he continuing to lose height but the rate of loss of it was accelerating. Puzzled enough to have even his growing panic checked he pulled the control column even further back. But the response was diametrically opposed to what it should have been. His speed grew faster still, his altimeter showed a continuing loss of height. Baffled he stared at the control column now pulled back well beyond the vertical. By all the laws which governed flight he should have been climbing steeply, there might even be risk of stalling! He pulled back further still — yet still the speed increased, still the altimeter needle continued its anti-clockwise course. Amazed he saw that the airspeed counter had travelled fully round the dial and was commencing its second turn, was indicating a speed significantly faster than that of normal level flight. His eyes flicked down to the altimeter: six hundred and fifty feet and falling, not just steadily but fast. He stared bewildered while his ears were filled with the sound of rushing night.

And then it came to him. There had been a vast miscalculation. There were circumstances in which the standard rules which governed flight ceased to apply. It explained so much. Others had met these circumstances — planes had vanished without trace and logical explanations had been sought to account for their disappearance. And this was all it was. How simple. How very simple. Allenby of eighteen course. Even Garland possibly. Suddenly they had found themselves as he was now — a Phaeton no longer in control. He watched the dials and a curious dispassion came over him. The speed was faster still, the height below five hundred feet with the altimeter needle having passed through the lowest point on the dial now moving evenly upwards, moving up to zero feet. He realised that very soon he would be dead. There would be a second muffled thump and a second ball of yellow flame that evening and if it so happened that his crash was near the airfield, those still due to fly would quit dispersal and put up with the cold to stare for a few moments at his funeral pyre — as he had stared at Garland's. And what was interesting was that of a sudden fear was quite gone. The situation was unchangeable; he had done what he'd been taught to do and done it, he was sure, correctly. If the Gods chose to play a little game sometimes and alter the rules of flight so that aircraft did the exact reverse of what they should be doing, ordinary mortals had no choice but to accept the consequences of their little joke.

Inexplicably the cheerful colours of the cockpit lights put him in mind of a cocktail party he had once attended. He couldn't quite see the connection yet the sense of it was very real. He leaned back against the seat, enjoying the recollection. It was not that he could actually bring to mind visions of other people, see the faces of men or girls he'd briefly met, it was just that the noise he could hear and the gay friendly lights about him were strangely analagous to the hum of conversation and the colours to the colours of drinks in glasses and their warmth to the feeling of companionship. Yet at the same time this was curious because the sound was anything but the same, for this sound was the scream of slipstream along the fuselage — a sound which, it seemed to him, was of a moving thing which would never stop but would continue into the endlessness of time when all there would be left of him would be bloody bits of bone mingled with cogs and wires and twisted metal.

And he experienced a calm he could not

remember experiencing before. In a few moments he would be dead — and it hardly seemed worth the effort to wonder what dying would be like.

★ ★ ★

He allowed his eyes to drift across the instruments — and all at once saw that the artificial horizon had toppled, the turn and bank was at a crazy angle and the gyro-compass spinning so fast its figures were indecipherable. For perhaps fifty of his precious remaining feet he stared open-mouthed, shaken from his torpor, seeing his machine as it really was, not as some uncontrollable meteor hurled by the Gods but as a Master aircraft tight-turning in a dipping circle, its navigation lights cutting a falling path like the coil of a spring. What he had done was utterly simple. Neglecting his instruments he had, unknowingly, put on bank; failing to keep the nose up with top rudder it had dropped and a gentle turn begun. By pulling back on the control column, far from correcting this he had merely tightened the turn and thus increased the speed and loss of height still further. In daylight, even at night with a good horizon, correction would have been instinctive, automatic, but with nothing against which to relate himself and his mind occupied with anything but what it should have been, his presumed corrections had merely snowballed the original error. The elevators were no longer acting to raise the nose but had become rudders tightening the turn and the more the turn was tightened the less lift the mainplanes provided. Had he but known it, at that moment it was a toss-up whether he would have crashed while still in his diving turn or as the result of flicking into an incipient spin.

His reaction was instinctive and immediate. With both hands clamped hard on the control column he hauled it sideways, taking off the bank. His mind was very clear for there hadn't been time for returning fear to cloud it and thoughts of death were banished. He must, he knew, be very careful. The altimeter showed a mere two hundred and fifty feet; only exquisite judgement could extract him from his predicament. Fighting the temptation to do otherwise, he pushed forward on the stick. Hauled back as it had been the turning would have been translated into a sudden climb with the risk of stall; yet at the same time the Master was in a falling pattern which the correction of the controls would not immediately amend. There was a sinking factor which it took time to overcome. Taking his left hand off the control column he shoved the throttle forward to its maximum position increasing boost, and, feeling the welcome surge of power, brought back the stick the merest trifle. Now there was little to do but wait — and hope. He dared not look at his altimeter; he did not look at it. Instead he concentrated on his turn and bank. The one thing he could do to assist his survival was keep the Master level; the rest lay with the Gods. And he knew there were only moments left in which his fate would be decided. Either his corrections had been taken in time for the downward drift to be halted or he would belly into the land or sea below.

4

Hands rammed into his greatcoat pockets, Shipman watched. Although the time since take-off was half a lifetime so far as Mitchell was concerned, in fact it was still only a matter of minutes, and the time between his going round again and now still less. Consequently by turning to port as sharply as he had and keeping the turn going long enough to feel sure the mountains must be behind his back, he had actually brought the Master back to a point where, when he began his tight diving turns, he was over the very sand dunes where Garland had killed himself little more than two hours previously.

Realising from the sound of it that something serious was amiss, Flying Officer Shipman had hastily squeaked back his chair and hurried out followed by the majority of the pupils yet to fly, to be greeted by the sight, crisply illuminated by its red and green wingtip lights, of an aircraft performing the most amazing gyrations. Experienced pilot though he was, as he was later to remark in the mess, he had never seen the like of it nor ever hoped to again. Anything but a case-hardened man (he loathed his drafting to Montrose as an instructor) he had been only too conscious when Garland had killed himself that it was he who had sent him out to his death and after it had happened had taken it on himself to suggest to the Station Commanding Officer that flying should be suspended for that night. Unable to prevail, he now faced the awful prospect of a repeat calamity about which he could do absolutely nothing.

The snarl of the Master's Kestrel engine drowned that of the surging sea and the biting wind chilled him unheeded. He was oblivious to the knot of youngsters standing aghast a yard or two behind him. His head moving to follow its terrifying arcs, he stared with fascinated horror at the ghastly, yet comical performance being executed before his very eyes. Not for an instant did it occur to him that Mitchell had the least hope of surviving and curiously his mind was occupied more with calculating how many turns he would make before he killed himself. But then it occurred, hopefully, to him, that perhaps the Master was unoccupied, that Mitchell had for some reason baled out. And the more he considered this possibility, the more he came to believe in it, so that he was torn between waiting for the crash or hurrying back into the dispersal hut to alert the station. And then, as if magically, the Master righted itself, and taking a course roughly reciprocal to its take-off run, its engine snarling even louder, skimmed over the top of the sand dunes and, beginning a gentle climb, headed northwards.

Shipman stared after it wonderingly; it would have been hardly less credible had some phantom aircraft performed what he had seen performed. He shook his head, his eyes still following the fading lights. Only then did he become aware of the gabble of voices from behind him. He turned swiftly: 'Get inside! All of you!' He had no idea why he gave the order or why he should be angry with them. And then he saw the yellow light spilling out from the opened door of the dispersal hut and yelled: 'And shut that door after you! Don't you know there's a bloody war on!'

They went unwillingly and when someone shut the door and he found himself abruptly plunged into blackness he regretted having given the order. Still watching the receding navigation lights and listening to the receding engine hum, he searched for cigarettes and having with some difficulty lit one he stayed out on the desolate, windswept, snow-scattered airfield trying to collect his thoughts.

'Do you know who's in that kite?'

He wheeled round disbelievingly. 'Who's that?'

'Corporal Rivers.'

'Rivers? Rivers?' And then he remembered. Rivers was that damned attractive Waaf who often ferried the pupils over for flying training.

'Yes,' he told her. 'His name's Mitchell.'

'Mitchell,' she said. 'Oh.' She said it very softly so that he could hardly hear the word. Yet a curious fatalism in it did not escape him.

'Is he a friend of yours?'

'No, not really.' And, after a pause. 'Could I have a cigarette?'

'I don't see why not.'

'Would you mind lighting it for me.'

He hesitated. It wasn't done for an other rank Waaf to, in effect, instruct an officer as she was doing. But it was a curious night. And besides she sounded anything but an other rank. And he remembered now she'd been discussed more than once in the mess. 'Damn shame she's not commissioned,' Radley had said. 'Wouldn't mind having a crack at her at all.' 'If she was commissioned you'd be killed in the rush,' someone had answered. And there'd been laughter.

He lit a second cigarette from his own and handed it to her.

'Thank you. Do you think he'll be all right?'

'God knows.'

'Any idea what was going wrong?'

'Not a clue.' And after a moment. 'Not a bloody clue.' He could see her face in the cigarette glow as she drew on it.

'Why was he sent round again?'

'Lord knows.'

'You weren't out here? When he was finishing his circuit?'

He took that for criticism.

'Corporal Rivers,' he said severely. 'If I stood out here and watched every pupil finishing his circuit on nights as cold as this one, it wouldn't be long before I was in Cortachy Castle with pneumonia. And an occasional 'Sir' wouldn't come amiss.'

'I'm sorry . . . Sir.'

'That's all right. We're all under a bit of strain. And you'd better not stand out here much longer or you'll be in Cortachy Castle.'

Yellow light spilled out suddenly from the hut. Figures were framed by it. 'Sir,' someone called. 'The C.O. wants you on the phone.'

He hadn't heard the ring although there was no reason now, except perhaps the wind and the surging surf, why he shouldn't have done.

'Coming!' he called back. And to the girl.

'You come in too.'

He turned his back on her and only when he turned to shut the door saw she hadn't obeyed, that she was standing, cigarette in mouth, looking in the direction of the departed Master. He hesitated, said 'Blast!' And, slamming the door shut behind him crossed to the kitchen table and picked up the telephone, paused, covered it with a hand and called to the nearest pupil: 'Get someone to start up another kite! Pronto!' He uncovered the receiver. 'Flying Officer Shipman.'

'What the hell's going on?'

'I don't know, Sir.'

'What sort of answer is that supposed to be?'

He controlled growing anger with difficulty. 'I don't know how to answer you, Sir,' he said. 'I've never seen anything like it in my life.'

'Anything like what?'

He realised that the Group Captain had no details, was merely aware that something was amiss.

'Like watching a pupil on his first night solo doing split-arse turns at a couple of hundred feet with sand dunes best part of a hundred and fifty feet high below him. Sir.'

260

'Jesus!' And after a moment. 'You know who it is?'

'Of course, Sir. Leading aircraftsman Mitchell.'

'Who approved him going solo?'

'I did. He did three night landings with me perfectly on Monday.'

'How many solo?'

'None. If you remember, Sir, the weather closed in.' With a feeling of dismay he waited for the question: 'Do you think it was very wise letting him go solo after a three day gap without at least one refresher dual circuit?' But it didn't come.

'How do you rate him? Mitchell?'

'Very promising.'

'Is he on the circuit now? I can't hear anything from here.'

This was wasting time. 'Last thing I saw of him he was heading for Aberdeen. Is it all right now' — he couldn't resist it — 'if I cancel flying for the night?'

There was a pause. 'Do that, will you?'

'I'd like to go and look for him. Is that approved, Sir?'

'Approved. I'll ready the landing lights.'

'Thank you, Sir.' When he put the telephone down he saw through the haze of smoke across the dozen or so faces all turned his way, eager young men with fresh cheeks nipped pink by the cold outside, all in flying gear, half at least with cigarettes in hand or mouth. He wondered exactly what he'd said to Brooker. 'Flying's cancelled,' he snapped. 'There's a Waaf outside freezing to death who'll take you back.'

5

Mitchell's gut reaction to eluding death by a hairsbreadth was to put as much space between himself and the ground as possible. His eyes glued to the instrument panel darted from turn and bank to altimeter to rate of climb to airspeed indicator like those of a cornered animal seeking some avenue of escape and in a plethora of impatience he prayed for the artificial horizon he had toppled in his wild manoeuverings to right itself as eventually it would.

Events crowding one on top of another and the sheer concentration he was applying to the immediate things on hand blotted out the sense of relief he might otherwise have felt at finding himself still alive. He did not for the moment even consciously think in terms of being in an aircraft at all, of there being a night outside, of the existence of other humans — the world had shrunk to the story being told by two square feet of metal plate pierced by six circular dials and the relationship of the story they were telling to his hands on throttle and control column and his feet on rudder bar. His body was ramrod tense, as were his bent arms and legs; this was not out of apprehension but because having once found how to hold the pointers in the required positions he locked his limbs to keep them exactly there. In effect both mentally and physically he made of himself a robot.

With a kind of grim satisfaction he saw the altimeter crawling upwards. For some reason the magic height to be reached was one thousand feet and it was only when this had been attained that peripheral thoughts began to intrude. The first of these was the realisation that he hadn't the least idea of where in the world — or more as it seemed to him, where in the universe — he was; and the second, which swiftly ousted the first, where the Grampians were. Well, he advised himself, the thing to do is to continue for the time being exactly as I am until, if I haven't hit them first, I've cleared them. He couldn't remember exactly how high they rose except that it wasn't above four thousand feet. Nevertheless for good measure, he decided to climb to five.

Thinking revived apprehension but the lessons learnt from the result of allowing fear to rule now enforced a better discipline. Stiff as an automaton, head thrust forward almost to the windscreen as if its being two or three inches nearer would give him that little extra time for taking evasive action, oblivious to the engine's note or drop in temperature as he climbed, he stared at his own eyes reflected in the Perspex canopy and braced his body for the half-expected collision. When it failed to come and the altimeter tidily confirmed the objective had been achieved, for the first time he relaxed and levelling out took stock of the situation.

It was, as he saw it, a pretty hopeless one. He had been flying, he imagined, for about half an hour (in fact it was far less) and he might be anything up to a hundred miles distant from Montrose, perhaps even more. Below him would almost certainly be either snow-capped mountain tops or a cold grey sea and there was no possible way of discovering which it was of these two equally unpleasant alternatives. Nor was there any way he could communicate with the world below or for the world below to communicate with him. In plain he was on his own a mile up in the sky, hopelessly lost with a limited time to find the answer before he ran out of fuel.

He could of course bale out — but the prospect of ending his life in the slow, solitary death of exposure on a mountain top or by drowning in an icy sea were both equally appalling. In any case he had begun to feel a bond between himself and the machine which, while everything else was beyond his power to control, was responsive to his commands and the thought of abandoning the comfort and reassurance of his comparitively warm and well-lit cockpit and projecting himself alone into the inhospitable empty darkness was anything but appealing.

He thought of God. But he was an unbeliever. He had tried hard to believe if only to fit in with schoolfellows who apparently mostly did, but failed. He remembered a discussion with a man named Smith who had the nickname 'Aggie' (because his initials were A.G.) who had been quite devout. Aggie had rejected his atheism out of hand and assured him with sweeping confidence that the time would come when he would suddenly find himself facing a crisis and then he would discover that after all he did believe and he would call on God for help and it would be given. Well, he supposed, there was no harm in trying and he did in fact say out aloud: 'Well, God, if ever I need some help it's now. Just tell me what to do.' But he was aware there was no conviction in it and wasn't surprised when no voice instructed him nor angels' wings appeared out of the night to flutter him and aircraft safely down.

His state of mind was by now quite

different from anything in his previous experience. Accepting that within the hour he would almost certainly be dead, fear, if not entirely conquered, had been subdued by a fatalistic composure in which he was able to study calmly the possibilities still open to him and recall such advice as had been given during training.

'What are you supposed to do when lost?' he seemed to hear a voice asking him. And he answered aloud. 'You do a square search.' 'And what, Mitchell, is a square search exactly?' 'Well, you pick a direction in which to fly and keep on it for a fixed length of time, two minutes say, and then you turn through ninety degrees, fly for another two minutes, turn again and so on until you've done a box and are more or less back where you started from. Then you start making another box next to that one and so on until you find something that's going to solve your problem.' Yes, that was all very well — in daylight. But what was he searching for *now*? A glimmer of light? A glimmer of light could equally be escaping from the carelessly pulled blackout curtain of a lowland cottage or mountainside hut; or from some ship far out at sea!

No, he told himself, the only hope left to me is finding Montrose airfield. And if I can't do that then, horrible though the thought of it is, I'm going to have to bale out and hope to hell this Master doesn't crash-land on a hospital or something. So I've got what? He glanced at the fuel contents indicators, one for each wing tank. About half an hour or so, I suppose, he decided. Enough for about three square searches. All right, then that's what I'll do. Three square searches, two minutes each leg and then if I haven't spotted someone flashing an Aldis lamp at me or something, out I go into, and he said it aloud, 'into that bloody Stygian abyss!'

★ ★ ★

He was aided now by the artificial horizon which had recovered so that he had the mock aircraft to indicate the relationship of his Master to the invisible real horizon. But he made two mistakes; one of which he was to realise quite soon, the other not at all. The sensible thing would have been first to fly on a reciprocal course to that which he had taken on his long slow climb so as to locate himself approximately where he'd started out before beginning the first of his square searches. The problem was that having in fact little belief he was likely to achieve anything in, (as he said aloud) 'aimlessly tooling round the sky using up what little petrol I've still got,' but, grimly determined at least to do what his elders and betters had instructed, he determinedly put out of his mind everything but the job on hand, looked at the heading shown by the gyro compass, glanced at the time of flight clock, and banking the Master into a meticulously rate one turn, held it thus for precisely ninety degrees before levelling out and setting off on his first of his four, two minute legs. It was only when halfway down the second of these he realised his error by which time compensating would have been far too complex a problem. If needs be, he thought, the first search has to be wasted; when its finished I'll do that reciprocal course for what? — well it was a guess, ten minutes — and then I'll start again.

The second mistake was caused by doing something which he ought to have done before and then goping over the top on it. Of a sudden, thinking about glimmers of light or Aldis lamps flashing at him from below, he realised that he'd be more likely to see them if he dimmed his cockpit lights to the minimum. And, having done this and been rewarded by the merciful disappearance of his own reflection in the hood, he decided to make an ever better job of it by switching off his navigation lights.

Now, for the first time since he had taken off, he had time to meditate. The comparitive warmth of the cockpit, the steady engine hum, the flickering exhaust flames, the dim glow of the navigation instruments, the reality of control column to his hand and rudder bar to his feet, the growing conviction that while it was sensible to do what he was doing there was really little purpose in it, the very feeling of being cut off from earthly influences, combined to create a frame of mind in which were elements of resignation, self-criticism and regret. He was sure he was going to die and was saddened more than afraid. There were so many things he had yet to do, so many ambitions unfulfilled. And the greatest of these perhaps, was to break his duck. He thought of girls he had known and soon of Corporal Rivers, the last girl he had seen or would ever see — or rather, he corrected himself, the last woman: for she seemed to him immeasurably more mature than he could ever be himself. He was, he admitted, a loner — which is to say that although he might be tolerated, he did not fit in easily; with any group of men he was always on the margin. And Corporal Rivers, it seemed to him, was something of a loner too, a misfit, if in a different way. She ought to have been commissioned which made her, in his eyes, superior to and separated from the Waafs she had to spend her time with. Far from being the only female he had ever found remotely attractive in Waaf uniform, she was quite lovely — which too set her apart. Again, except for the vague hints that she was lesbian — which he didn't really understand — there were no sexual rumours spread about her as there were about so many of the other Waafs.

It did not occur to him to carry the image further. His nature was such as to have him divide women into two categories: those one could have sex with and those who were not so much untouchable as not to be touched. From the first he drew the sexual fantasies with which he filled his mind; from the second the romantic concepts on which he based his aspirations. The two were to be kept rigidly separate and thus he was with girls invariably confused — and usually ineffective. Those who made it clear they were only too willing to let him do to them what his lusts slyly urged, repelled him; those who met the impossibly high standards he set for himself (without ever seriously imagining they *would* be met) found him tongue-tied and disappointing. On the few occasions when girls of deeper perception *had* wondered if there wasn't perhaps rather more in Harry Mitchell than he was given credit for, the chance of such acquaintanceships burgeoning had withered on the vine of his own unsureness.

And so the idea of considering Julie Rivers either sexually or with familiarity hardly crossed his mind; she merely rested there briefly, comfortingly, companionably — until his thoughts shifted elsewhere.

He wouldn't get his wings after all. That was the next most important ambition which would be unfulfilled. From inspection he knew that a pilot's brevet opened doors which had been closed, admitted one to a brotherhood envied by all who could not be part of it, gave the wearer self-assurance and so far as girls were concerned worked magic. There was much of the Walter Mitty in Harry Mitchell and he had seen himself fully-fledged, smart in uniform, sergeant's or officer's, brevet on breast ordering dinner and wine in romantic restaurants while across candlelit tables pretty girls in off the shoulder evening dresses gazed at him adoringly. Well it was not to be; not that, nor the daredevil exploits in Spitfire or Hurricane, or the long tense flights over enemy territory in Halifax or Lancaster, nor the binges with his kind in the Regent Palace Hotel in Piccadilly which was apparently where aircrew met on leave, nor any of the other vague imaginings which had filled his daydreams. It was not to be, none of it, because he'd made a mess of things. He'd been given his chance and botched it. Had been so focussed on managing the simple matter of raising a Master's flaps as to have completely overlooked the possibility of disorientating himself. And having got lost had all but crashed by ignoring a bevy of instruments there to tell him him exactly what he was doing. The simple fact of the matter, he told himself, was that he was in this, as he had shown himself in so many other ways, inept. He'd had no business putting himself forward as aircrew and in the extremely unlikely event he by some miracle survived he would have himself reclassified.

This train of thoughts occupied his mind through his first square search and along the reciprocal leg of his climb away from Montrose and by an odd coincidence he had just reached this decision when he saw the flare. It was faint and far away, a greenish glow which grew, hesitated, fell away in a curious trajectory and died. He did not at once connect it with himself, in fact saw it rather as in normal times he might have seen a shooting star; it was only when after a interval of perhaps two minutes he saw another, this time nearer and seeming to climb higher up towards him, that he realised what it was. That someone was firing cartridges from a Very pistol.

The events of his traumatic first night solo had combined to give a disproportionate relevance to everything with which he was concerned as had been evidenced by the almost puritanical precision of his flying from the moment when he had recovered self-control; as soon as he saw the flare for what it was, a homing beacon, in much the same way as a penitent reads approval in subsequent happenings which benefit him, so Mitchell saw a direct connection between it and his decision to have himself reclassified as groundstaff. It was as if the Gods objecting to an incompetent careering round their firmament and determined to be rid of him had unbent on discovering he was going to quit it voluntarily.

It all made sense to Mitchell and dissipated the last shreds of fear. It did not occur to him that the tremendous stresses he had borne were still affecting him nor that he was actually handling the aircraft now with greater expertise than he had ever handled one before; even had he done so he would have failed to see there was an arrant contradiction between this and his decision to be done with flying. And the experience which still lay ahead before he finally put the

Master safely down on Montrose airfield would do nothing but reinforce an obstinate conviction.

★　★　★

Inexperienced airline passengers are confused, and often quite alarmed, when, on a flight made at night, their pilot, following unknown ground instructions, instead of making a direct approach circles the airfield at a lowish level. Instead of their first sight of the flare path being a line of brilliant lights beside which they will very shortly touch down, they may suddenly see this necklace above the level of their heads seeming to indicate they are flying if not upside down at least in the most peculiar of attitudes. And as they watch their sense of disorientation increases as this line of lights, appearing to be a moveable axis continually changes its direction, sometimes as it were diving underneath the aircraft, at others angled upwards to the heavens. The explanation is of course quite simple: however steep the bank of their aircraft, securely strapped in in their seats and with the world outside their tiny windows black, everything they see around them appears to be on a level and horizontal plane while anything they may chance to see outside the aircraft which is in fact horizontal appears to be at an angle of some sort. But then by some magic the pilot sorts things out, persuades the flare path to behave itself and lie down decently where it ought to, makes his approach and lands. Apprehension is set aside and in the business of extracting hand baggage and inching uncomfortably towards the exit doors, soon forgotten. And after a few more night landings the passenger gets the hang of things and accepts, or even loses all interest in what is no longer a phenomenon.

Mitchell on his second attempt to put the Master down was in a similar, but somewhat worse situation in that instead of being able to comfort himself with the reflection that however odd things seemed to be, here were a few hundred fellow passengers who were clearly quite at ease and that instead of there being somewhere up front a trained crew (who must obviously know what they were doing or they'd have killed themselves long ago) he was alone. He had been trained to fly on instruments and to expect his first sight of the flare path to be at a time when he was more or less flying parallel to it and descending at an angle onto which he'd been directed by the glide path indicator. Now, as he changed his course and steeply dropped the aircraft's nose to head directly towards the latest signal, he suddenly saw, as if by magic, a row of pearls appear in the sky above him. Unknown to him Montrose was equipped with a perfectly normal peace time flare path and in the desperate circumstances that some fool of a pupil was blundering around up above obviously lost and at his wits end to know what to do, the station Commanding Officer had no alternative but to 'risk the presence of a stooging Dornier or Heinkel and turn the blasted things full on!'

Astonished by this sudden manifestation, Mitchell stared at it for some moments before recognizing it for what it had to be and at once, instinctively (as well might have the tryo airline passenger had he been in Mitchell's flying boots) put on bank and climb to compensate. But now in his state of numbed calm very much on the alert so far as his instruments were concerned he soon realised his error and, correcting it, restored the chain of lights more or less to their original position.

This, however, merely delayed rather than removed the problem. With four thousand feet to lose before getting down to the proper circuit height the question of making a direct approach and landing did not arise and long before he was sufficiently low, he had passed over the flare path and it had vanished below the belly of the Master and when he banked to bring it into view again it was to discover it now running in a totally different and quite perplexing direction. And so for quite some time it continued. Whenever he changed his aircraft's altitude the row of lights gyrated crazily. Now they ran from some point in the sky to disappear beneath him as if into some hole in the ground; now momentarily, they vanished only to reappear on his other side. Sometimes when he forced them straight and parallel, they were too high and seemed to be running level with him, or even above so that he was looking up at them, whilst at others they stretched ahead like an angled hill. He realised where the problem lay but found it extraordinarily difficult to divorce himself from looking at it back to front. He could not rid himself of the feeling he was fixed and the lights were moving. Even while he understood perfectly clearly that all that was required was the application of common-sense, he found himself trying to solve the enigma as if it were one of the exercises in three dimensional geometry he had found difficult at school.

Aware that by now he must be running low on fuel, he steeled himself to find the answer and eventually, almost accidentally placing the flare path in a relationship with himself he could grapple with, saw how to do so. Of a sudden everything slotted into place and the puzzle was a simple one to solve, indeed not a puzzle any longer. He had passed through the barrier of confusion and in doing so, become a relatively experienced night flying pilot. Meticulously correct at the very end he did not immediately attempt to force the Master down but flew at the stipulated one thousand feet above the flare path, made the necessary turns, across, down and across wind again, lowered undercarriage and flaps at the proper times and picking up the glide path indicator, switched on his landing lights, made a respectable landing and taxied to the dispersal point.

★ ★ ★

None of this changed his view of things. He had made an utter fool of himself and by the morning there wouldn't be a soul on the station who wasn't aware of it; his standing amongst his fellow pupils, always suspect, would be rock bottom. By some miracle he had escaped disaster and it would be both ungrateful and idiotic to imagine he would do so a second time. Climbing out of the cockpit he paused for a moment to stare up at the inky sky. A line or two of Air Force doggerel crossed his mind: *Only birds and fools fly, and birds don't fly at night.* How true that is, he thought — but the difference is that this fool isn't going to fly by daylight either. And wrenching the helmet from his head he turned, ready to face the strictures.

★ ★ ★

They were brief. Squadron Leader Wilkie, (not the Station Commander but O. C. Intermediate Training Squadron, No. 8. Flying Training School, Montrose), was waiting for him. He had given strict orders that no one else should speak to Leading Aircraftsman Mitchell who would obviously be in a distressed, if not overwrought condition.

'Come in for a moment, Mitchell,' he ordered.

Mitchell followed him into the bare, cold, empty dispersal hut.

'Are you all right?'

'Yes, Sir.'

'Do you want to talk about it?'

'I'd rather not, Sir.'

Wilkie thought he understood. The boy was shellshocked; there'd be a reaction later. He remembered being told that the worse thing was to bottle up such experiences. That the best thing to do was talk them through; not dwell on them in solitude. He set about saying as much.

'I can see that, Mitchell,' he said. 'But you know . . . ' He paused, searching for the most helpful words.

'I'm sorry to have been such a nuisance, Sir,' Mitchell said.

Wilkie nodded gratefully. 'Well you have been rather.' He pointed to the ceiling. 'Flying Officer Shipman's still up there looking for you and I don't mind telling you, you nearly gave us all down here heart failure.' He hesitated but could not resist it. 'When you were carrying out those most impressive steep diving turns, do you know where you were?'

'No, Sir.'

'Over the sand dunes. You must have cleared them by fifty feet at best. Remarkable. You're a very lucky man.' He felt he had gone off the rails and missed his opportunity. 'Best thing you can do,' he suggested gruffly, 'is get your chums to bring you a couple of double scotches and then get a good night's sleep. We'll talk about it in the morning.'

Had it been Shipman with him in the dispersal hut, Mitchell would have told him his decision. He thought about telling Wilkie now but his dizzy rank defeated him.

'Yes, Sir,' he said.

'Okay. Cut off now. There's a Waaf outside in a Commer who insisted on being here to take you over.' He was quite sure there was nothing in it, that the girl was too lovely and experienced for there to be anything between her and this immature and not particularly impressive youngster — but he wanted to lighten the situation and add a little to Mitchell's self-esteem. 'She's very pretty. You're a lucky young bugger, you know,' he ended.

6

'Well done,' she said.

He laughed derisively. 'Well done?'

'Well it was well done.'

'An hour? To do one landing?'

She forced a chuckle. 'It must have felt like half a dozen.' His sang-froid had thrown her. Expecting him to be agitated and irresolute, ready to be sympathetic and understanding, his self-assurance was bewildering. It was as if the nervous boy she had driven across had been changed into quite another human being. 'At any rate,' she went on, 'you've certainly got some night flying time to put in your Log Book. You must have more than anyone in your course.'

'I suppose so.'

His apathy robbed her of words. They drove in silence across the width of the airfield. As she turned the Commer at its end, she said: 'I'll drive you to your mess.'

'It'll be all right if you drop me off at my billet.'

'But you'll want to celebrate still being in the land of the living, won't you?'

'No. No, I don't feel like doing that.'

'But they'll be expecting you. Your chums.' And she came out with it. 'Don't you realise, Harry, you've had the whole station agog. Holding its breath. We were all out watching. They'll be *waiting* for you. Waiting to hear all about it, what it was like and . . . well, all the rest of it. They'll be hanging on your words. They'll be . . . '

'By which,' he interrupted, 'you mean that normally I'm of no account but just for the moment because I've done a Prune, I'm a bit of a celebrity. Don't worry. It won't last. Anyway I'm done with flying.'

'Why are you so bloody sorry for yourself?'

'I'm not in the least sorry for myself. Just drop me off at my billet.'

'But you'll want to celebrate still being in the land of the living, won't you?'

'No. No, I don't feel like doing that.'

She tried another tack. 'Harry, you mustn't miss the opportunity of going to your mess and shooting the best line you can about this while it's fresh enough in their minds for people to want to listen to you. You'll be making the biggest mistake of your life.' And when he didn't respond. 'Listen to me, Harry, for reasons I'm not going to tell you, I know what I'm talking about. You don't realise it but you're in a state of shock. And no wonder. I think *I'd* be in hysterics. But it's

284

not hit you in that way. Although it probably will when you come out of this . . . this *mood* you're in. All right. Miss your opportunity. Don't go and join all those chaps who're waiting for you. But for heaven's sake don't do anything drastic about your flying.' A thought struck her. 'You haven't done so already, have you? You didn't say all this to Squadron Leader Wilkie.'

'No. I didn't have the guts to. If it'd been Shipman, I would have. I'm going to tell *him* in the morning.' He made a curious sound, an expellation of air from his chest. 'Huh! He's up there, you know! Looking for me!'

'You don't have to worry about him . . . '

'I'm not. That's the whole point of what I'm saying. It won't present any problem to him. Finding the airfield. Putting her down.' He became quite formal. 'No, Miss. It's kind of you to take this interest. Don't think I don't appreciate it. But I've quite made up my mind. That flight was the last I'll ever make, except as a passenger . . . So if you wouldn't mind running me to my billet.'

She felt quite desperate. It could not be left like this. It might have been a curate's egg of a first night solo but amongst the shenanigans there'd been some very competent flying. And swift reactions. But that was not the point — whether or not the boy would make

285

a skilful pilot. There were far more important things at stake.

'Harry,' she said, 'before I do, will you answer just one question? Honestly. Will you do that? Will you tell me what were the important things you weren't going to do if you killed yourself? The things you were thinking about up there?' And when he stayed silent. 'Getting your wings was one, wasn't it?'

'Yes.' He spoke grudgingly.

'And what else? Was there anything else?' She put her hand back on his thigh. 'There was something else, wasn't there?' She felt him shifting in discomfort. 'Yes, there was, wasn't there? Only it's something you don't want to talk to me about. Well you don't have to. But giving up flying's not going to help that either, is it?' She finished abruptly, and started the engine. As she did so, she saw the navigation lights of an aircraft far in the distance. 'That's Flying Officer Shipman, coming back,' she said. 'I'll run you to your billet so that you won't have the discomfort of watching him make a perfect approach and landing.'

7

He checked the blackout carefully then switched on the hard, bright light. The stove was almost out and the billet was very cold; Garland's bed not yet made up for sleeping, the blankets tidily folded and stacked on the metal frame, was depressing. He shivered, raked the fire and added coals from the small box beside it. He decided against taking off sidcot and flying boots until the chill had lessened. He lit a cigarette and sat on the edge of his own bed smoking it, looking about him. Until now he had thought the billet with its stove, its pair of beds, their few personal belongings, the gramophone, the pairs of strings running to each bedhead, a cosy place, far preferable to the long narrow huts like hospital wards which most of the course had to put up with. Now with Garland dead, with his empty bed seeming to accuse him of disloyalty by being still alive, it had lost its charm. Well, he told himself, it doesn't matter, it's only for tonight. When I remuster they'll have me out. His eyes surveying the room fell on the photographs on the low locker in which Garland kept his things. He got to his feet and studied them one after the other: Garland in blazer and white flannels, hands nonchalantly in his pockets with his parents and his brother, his mother's arm tucked through his own, his father's around his brother's shoulder; Garland and a girl friend in the front seats of the family car, a Morris with the hood slung back; another girl with wavy hair and an eager smile. He'd lied to Corporal Rivers when he'd claimed Garland as a friend. They'd got on tolerably well together, shared a billet, even gone on a drunken binge to Dundee over Hogmanay. But they hadn't been really friends, hadn't had enough in common — not with their different backgrounds. He came back to the family snap. It said it all, he was thinking, when he heard the soft rap on the door. Guiltily, he put the photograph back, switched off the light and, cigarette in hand, opened the door.

'Who is it?' he said.

'Me.' His mouth opened in astonishment and disbelief. She pushed past him, into the billet. 'Well shut the door. Put the light on.'

He did so wonderingly. She looked about her, quickly taking in the little there was to see, then going to the stove put her hands towards it. 'It's cold,' she said.

'I've stoked it up.'

'I mean't outside. It's not cold in here. Not in comparison. Can I have one, please?'

He realised what she meant. 'Oh. Yes.' He offered her his case. It had been his last birthday present from his mother and had a built in lighter in one corner. He was very proud of owning it. It had flair. He flicked the lighter. Cigarette in mouth she bent her head, drew smoke in expertly and blew it out.

'Thank you, Harry.' With her free hand she took off her cap and put it down on Garland's bed, shook out her hair a little.

'Why . . . why have you come?' he asked.

'To keep you company. You're not safe leaving on your own. How on earth did you manage this?'

'What?'

'Getting a billet like this?'

'I don't know. It just came up. I think there's four of them altogether and we got this one allocated to us. Me and Garland. Just the luck of the draw, I suppose.'

'What are those strings for?'

'To open the stove door when you're in bed. Or to close it.'

'What fun! Your idea?'

'No, Garland's. He's a clever chap . . . Was.'

'Show me how it works.'

'Oh . . . All right.' He demonstrated. She

looked admiringly at the way it did work, the strings running up and over screw-in brass hooks so that the angles would be correct.

'That really is very clever,' she said. She looked at the record on the gramophone. 'Stardust. How lovely. Put it on, Harry.' She sat on Garland's bed.

'Well . . . ' It seemed indecent. 'It isn't my gramophone.'

'He didn't mind you playing it?'

'Well, no . . . but.'

'He wouldn't mind. I'm sure he wouldn't.' He still hesitated. 'If you don't put it on, then I will. It's one of my favourites.'

'Oh, all right.'

His hand was trembling and he had difficulty placing the needle in the starting groove correctly and scraped over the first bar or two. He glanced at her guiltily but she didn't appear to have noticed. The hand holding her cigarette was lowered by her side and its smoke drifted lazily upwards. Her head was cocked a little to one side as she listened attentively. When the vocal began she said: 'Bing,' rather dreamily. And when he made to respond: 'Shh!'

When the record came to its end, she said: 'What's on the other side?'

'The pessimistic character with the crab apple face.'

'No! Not after Stardust. What a funny choice.'

'Yes. It is, isn't it?'

'How's the fire? No. Let me do it.' The strings, two pairs which began in tandem, were arranged so that the ends of each pair ran to the head of each bed where they were tied. 'Here, get rid of this. I don't really want it.' She handed him her cigarette and lying back over the pile of folded blankets, reached for the string and plucked it. Obediently the stove door swung open. 'That really is very clever,' she said. 'And the fire's doing well. Turn the light off, Harry. Let's be cosy. Turn the light off and then put Stardust on again. Oh, I suppose you need the light. Put it on first and then switch off the light.'

He was quite out of his depth. His heart was thumping absurdly and for all that in his fantasies he'd conjured up imaginary situations no less outlandish than this one was, he was desperately nervous.

'Suppose someone comes?' he ventured.

'What if they do?'

'You wouldn't mind . . . I mean . . . Well being caught in here with me?'

'I'm not,' she said, 'exactly in *flagrante delicto*.'

It was a new expression to him but he got the gist of it. 'Well, no,' he stumbled. 'But they might think . . . '

'What might they think?' Her tone was bold. 'Come on, Harry, what might they think?' She laughed softly. 'Go on, put it on.'

★ ★ ★

While the record was playing she lay back using the blankets as a pillow humming the tune some of the time when Crosby wasn't singing. The firelight threw shadows and gave life to the room. He stood uneasily by the gramophone not knowing what to do with himself yet fearful of the record coming to its end.

When it did, she said: 'These things are damned uncomfortable as mattresses, aren't they? My backside must look like a fishing net.' She sat up.

'Hadn't you better go?' he suggested. 'Before someone finds you're missing?'

'Go? I'm not going to go. I'm going to stay here all night with you.'

He gaped.

'I told you,' she said. 'You're not safe leaving on your own.' She stood. 'How are we going to organise this?' She was looking at Garland's bed. 'I know. Suppose we tip the beds up against the walls? That'll give us much more room. And if we tip yours up across the door, that'll give us time to get organised if anyone tries to come in.' She turned from the bed to look at him, smiling a little sadly. 'Harry,' she said, 'you're going to make love to me. I know you haven't done it before but you're going to do it now. I'm going to show you how.' She took the step or two across to him and put her hands up on his shoulders. 'Now, kiss me.'

He did so inexpertly, crushing his lips hard on hers, killing feeling. She pulled her head away.

'That's no good, Harry. Now do exactly as I tell you. Put your lips against mine gently but leave your mouth open. Now, kiss me again.'

He did so and felt her lips moving softly, making his move in concert and then the tip of her tongue tracing round his lips, inside and out, and then exploring deeper, seeking all the recesses of his mouth, folding over and under his own tongue. Although it was a new experience he knew what this was called: a *French Kiss*. There was a lot of talk about it and there were some who boasted it was the only way to kiss, that it was the only way they did kiss. You never knew whether or not to believe them.

She took her mouth away, still holding him at a little distance. Then dropped her hands.

'Wasn't that nicer?'

He gulped. 'Yes.' He seemed to have been taken into another world. His head was swimming and he had to put his hand on the bedhead to support himself.

'Turn the light on again, will you, Harry?' she said. 'Only for a minute. We'll have to get these knots undone.'

He realised she'd meant what she'd said about the beds. He was bemused, disbelieving, but totally overmastered. He switched on the light.

'You undo the other ones,' she said.

He obeyed and when they had both undone the knots, under her instructions they put pillows, sheets and blankets on the floor and then, first turning them round so that the legs were towards the walls, they stood the iron beds on their sides.

'There,' she said surveying the space they'd created, 'That'll be better, won't it? Which end do you think we ought to have the pillows? This end don't you think? So we can look into the fire.'

He watched in silence as she unfolded the blankets and sheets and made a presentable looking double bed on the wooden floor. 'Turn the light out,' she ordered him while doing this. 'And look, we won't want these extra sheets. Roll them up and put them along the bottom of the door to keep the draught out.'

In a state approaching mental stupefaction he did these tasks in the order she had instructed. Although sexually excited and with his heart beating so fast and strongly as to seem to blot out other sounds, he was dreading whatever lay ahead without for a moment contemplating there was a way of escaping it. Perplexed, embarrassed, ignorant of sex in all but its most general terms, overmastered by her obvious experience and her total self-assurance, he was putty in her hands unable to imagine any order she could give him he wouldn't at once carry out. He was glad of the draught excluders which had to be threaded in with difficulty behind his own bed now tilted on its edge against the wall and it was with regret he admitted to himself there was nothing better he could do with them and rose to face the ordeal ahead.

Without surprise he saw that she had already taken off her tunic and tie and put them both over the arm of the shabby old armchair Garland had rescued from some-where. Her fingers were busy undoing shirt buttons but seeing his eyes on her she paused.

'No girl's ever undressed for you before, Harry, have they?' she said.

'No.'

'You don't have to watch me if it's too embarrassing. Look, tell you what. Bank the fire up while I finish. I'll let you know when to turn round.'

'Yes.' With relief he turned away and made the slowest possible business of putting on coals. Even so when there was nothing more to do he could still hear small sounds behind him.

'All right, Harry,' he heard. 'You can turn round now.'

He turned slowly, fearfully.

She was lying naked on the bed she'd constructed on the floor in a pose calculated both to show her body to perfection and to strip away the least veneer of modesty. Her hands were by her sides, her feet were towards the fire and she had moved the pillows away so that her head was resting on the blankets stretching her neck and firming her breasts. One knee was raised deliberately.

'Take your clothes off,' she said. 'I won't watch you. I couldn't, could I, Harry? Not with my head back like this?'

He stared at her in awe. He had never seen a woman's breasts exposed before let alone her whole body. He hadn't known till now that pubic hair existed on a girl.

'Take your clothes off,' she said again as if

reading his thoughts. 'Don't worry. There's nothing to worry about.'

Forgetting he was wearing flying boots he started to take off his sidcot and had to sit with it half off his shoulders hindering his movements. His fingers were clumsy, fumbling. When it was managed and his things were scattered about him he stood scarlet-faced, ashamed of his rampant penis.

'All right?' he heard her say. 'May I look now?'

'Yes,' he whispered.

She raised her head.

'You're beautiful!' she said.

And he was. Long-legged, slim-hipped, wide-shouldered, the flickering firelight dancing on an unblemished body, his features were of a sudden of no account; or rather with his short but naturally wavy hair, his full lips parted, his eyes glowing with the desire he couldn't hide, they seemed, in their very immaturity, to be of one with it.

My God, she told herself, I must be careful.

'Come here,' she said. He came unwillingly. 'Kneel down. Here.' She patted the blanket. He obeyed. 'Now kiss me here. And here,' she said. And touched her nipples, one and then the other. 'And don't hurry. We've got all night.' She laid her head back deliberately to

297

tauten her nipples for his mouth. He bent his head. 'No, no,' she said. 'Not like that. Take it into your mouth and use your tongue on it. And bite it very gently with your teeth.'

But he had hardly begun to do as she had bidden him before she realised she'd have to stop him. No, this is wrong, she told herself. I'm like a schoolmaster's wife seducing one of his boys and whatever happens I mustn't lose control. She raised a hand and gently pushed his head away.

'Was it wrong? Did I do it wrong?'

'No, Harry, you did it beautifully.'

Besides he'd better fuck me now, she thought. He won't be able to hold on and then it'll all be messy.

She sat up.

'Listen to me, Harry. You're going to do it now and it'll probably be over very quickly for you. But that won't be the end, only the beginning. Do you understand? I won't be going when it's over. I'm going to stay all night. You understand?'

'Yes.' His voice was husky with despairing lust.

'Go on, then. I'll help you.' It needed every atom of will power to keep her voice calm and practical.

'But . . .'

'It's all right. You don't have to worry.'

'I mean . . . Well I haven't got any . . . '

'I know what you mean. And I know what you haven't got. It'll be all right. Just believe me.' If I explain, she thought, he probably won't even begin to understand. Besides . . .

Her own desire had become all but insupportable. She fought against it. 'All right,' she said. 'Go down there. That's right. Just a minute. Try taking some of the weight on your arms, you'll find it easier. Yes, that's it.' She took his penis in her hand and guided him into her. 'That's it,' she said. 'That's it.'

* * *

It was over for him very quickly. She could have matched him but it was essential if she was to achieve her purpose that she should retain her independence and superiority. She felt his weight fall on her and listened jealously to his gasps. When he would have pulled away, she stopped him. 'No,' she said. 'Stay inside me.' And she tightened her sphincter muscles to hold him in the way that Freddie had taught her. She put a hand on his head and ran it through his hair and felt it wet with sweat. Poor boy, she thought, what have I done? But she felt proud rather than guilty and anyway these thoughts were false thoughts intended to keep her from dwelling on her own needs. She alternately relaxed and tautened her muscles — it was something she and Freddie had learnt to do together and brought to such a fine art that she was able to make him come just by doing it. 'That's nice, Harry, isn't it?' she crooned. But again she had to stop because of what it was doing to herself. She let him go and rolled over on her front. 'Do you think I'm pretty, Harry. Tell me I'm pretty.' He mustn't be allowed to think too much about himself.

'You're lovely.'

'What parts of me do you like best?' She looked over her shoulder at him wickedly. He was kneeling now beside her and the fire was casting a moving shadow of his body and she could imagine it dancing upon her buttocks. Could remember lying so often on a sitting-room floor in front of a fire with Freddie. Forgive me, Freddie, she thought, I'm doing this for this boy. That's the only reason I'm doing it. And I can't help it if it arouses me. It's been so long. *You* under-stand. *You'll* understand if anyone does. 'Do you like this part?' She reached for his hand and put it on her buttocks. She remembered what Freddie had said, with a surprise in his voice which convinced her it was genuine, the first time she'd been naked with him: that the skin on her buttocks was like silk to touch.

'Tell me,' she said. 'You don't have to be shy with me any more.'

'Yes,' he said — and she sensed the first touch of strength in his voice. 'Yes. I like all of you.'

'You don't know all of me yet. But you will. Use both hands. And run them over my back. Gently. With your fingertips.'

She turned away from him and reaching for a pillow, rested her head on it and lay quite still enjoying the light touch of his exploring fingertips. When they reached the nape of her neck, she shivered.

'Are you cold?' He spoke hastily. 'I'll put more coal on if you're cold.'

'No, I'm not cold. Don't stop.'

She concentrated on the sensations his fingers were arousing — in some ways she found this skimming of fingers over her the most delicious part of sex. She closed her eyes willing him to extend his areas of exploration and gradually he did until there was nowhere he could reach he hadn't touched.

'All right, Harry,' she said. 'It's my turn now. Come and lie down and I'll do it to you. No, lie on your back.'

He obeyed and she knelt beside him and for a little while made circles with her fingertips on his chest and thighs and stomach, barely touching him, threatening all the time to bring her hands together on his penis and then at the last moment taking them apart again, watching him all the time. And when his erection came without her touching it, and he made some movement, she said: 'No, just lie there as you are. I'll do it to you this time.'

8

So she guided him through all the ramifications and varieties of sex which she and Freddie had mutually discovered and enjoyed. His young, healthy, sex-starved body responded eagerly urging her to throw all discipline aside and lose herself in an orgy of lust and satisfaction. She fought off temptation, persuading herself that so long as she resisted, so long as she retained her self-control and stayed teacher rather than participant, she was not destroying her husband's trust in her.

Until this night she had never been unfaithful. It was as a virgin she had come to Freddie and, more than that, as a virgin totally ignorant of the depth of sensualism which lay within her. It had not been Freddie who had developed it; it was something which had lain there within her, waiting dormant as a seed waits for nature's call. As the seed responds to sun and warmth so had her body responded to Freddie Rivers' love. And the explosion had been devastating. He had looked at her amazed, almost in awe, almost disbelieving, that in this quiet, reserved and lovely girl such depths of passion could possibly exist. Had it not been that he himself, if to a lesser degree, was a voluptuary their relationship would have been insupportable. As it was they had discovered that perfect unison in sex granted to so very few couples as to fill their lives with continual joy and satisfaction and keep them utterly without the need of others. No other man had ever attracted her; the possibility of extra-marital sex had hardly crossed her mind. If within their relationship there were no extremes, if there was nothing however imaginative, however bizarre, they wouldn't sample and, if enjoyed, repeat, outside of it their living was quite unsullied. Wherever he went, she went with him, sharing married quarters, accepting new postings uncomplainingly, casually enjoying the company of his friends, of other pilots, missing none of them when they moved on. Her life had been complete in Freddie's and his complete in her and flying. Only the war had brought them problems.

'If anything happens to me,' he had once said, half jokingly — and this before the war broke out — 'what are you going to do about this?'

'Find a bigger one,' she had joked in return.

'Yes, well I think that would be wise.'

'Don't be silly. Nothing's going to happen to you.'

'It only needs a bit of grit in the wrong place or some idle groundstaff wallah forgetting to tighten up a screw . . . '

'Don't talk about it.'

'That hurts.'

'It was meant to. You're not to talk like that. Never. I couldn't live without you.'

'You could live without *me*. But I'm damn sure you couldn't live without sex.'

'I managed perfectly well before I met you.'

'Only because you didn't know what you were missing.'

'How do I know what I'm not missing now?'

'What's that supposed to mean?'

'Perhaps I ought to try someone else. Just to see. Bill Hutchinson would oblige. When I . . . '

'You just try. I'll murder you.'

'Would you, Freddie? If I came home and told you I'd slept with someone else would you murder me?'

He thought about it. Became quite serious. 'Yes, I think I might.'

'Darling!' She had leaned over and kissed him lightly. 'How sweet of you. How would you do it? Would you strangle me to get it over quickly? Or would you do it slowly, with some pills or something . . . '

The conversation had drifted off into silliness but behind it there had been this element of gravity. If she wouldn't acknowledge openly that if she was parted from him for any length of time she would have a problem, she acknowledged it to herself. The doors of sex having been opened to her, her need would be an ever-pressing one. Yet to destroy his trust in her would be to destroy his belief in life.

The war separated them. For a couple of months she had existed seeing him only on his weekend leaves and then she had become a camp follower, staying in a hotel local to his station or renting rooms. And then one morning he had not come back. And after a day or two a letter had come telling her something she already knew, a letter on crisp parchment-coloured paper from the Air Ministry Casualty Branch: '*Madam, I am commanded by the Air Council to express to you their great regret on learning that your husband, Squadron Leader Frederick William Rivers D.F.C., Royal Air Force, is missing as the result of air operations on the night of March 5th, 1941 when the Wellington which he was commanding set out to bomb Kiel and was not heard from again. This does not necessarily mean that he has been killed or wounded . . . '* She had crushed the letter in despair, knowing the contents in advance, having heard them from his fellow pilots. But then, a few weeks later, had come a telegram followed by a confirming letter telling her he was alive, unhurt, a German prisoner of war and she had wept all morning for the joy of it.

She had decided what to do. Sooner or later she would be called up anyway, drafted into the Land Army or something else not of her choosing. She had volunteered for the Woman's Auxiliary Air Force. With her background and education, the wife of a serving and reasonably high ranking officer, she could almost certainly have obtained a commission. But she foresaw the problems of finding herself continually in the company of young men who thought as she thought, spoke as she spoke and would be like Freddie in so many ways. It would be easier, she calculated, to fight the battle she knew lay ahead in a life spent with other ranks. And so it had proved. And if the fire of sexual need still smouldered inside she had learnt to live with it.

★　★　★

Now, through what had begun as sympathy for an immature adolescent, she had fanned it furiously to life. At the beginning she had convinced herself that what she was doing was for a worthwhile purpose and by a considerable effort of will controlled the situation. But she had failed to take into account what might happen when her guard was lowered. Half-waking in the small hours of the morning nature had its say. 'Harry,' she whispered, hardly aware she was saying it. 'Harry!'

He grunted, worn out in mind, exhausted by her physically.

She clung to him, pressing herself against his back, running her hand down his front and thigh.

'Give it to me, Harry,' she begged him. 'Give it to me.'

He stumbled into half wakefulness. 'I don't know if I can.'

'Yes, you can. I'll help you.'

She used all her wiles, all her experience, and finally aroused him sufficiently for him to enter her. And at his entry a tremendous explosion of lust took over her. Many months of repressed desire overwhelmed all inhibition. She abandoned herself to him completely, all thoughts of Freddie, all thoughts of motive banished. She dug her nails into his back, she cried out in abandon, she writhed, she gasped, exulted. It was to him as if he held a serpent in his arms. She was a beggar in her demands, terrifying in her hunger, appalling in her speech, gratifying in her praise. For the first time with a girl he found himself the master.

When it was over, she said to him: 'Is that fire still alight?'

He examined it. 'Just about.'

'Can you do something with it?'

'Yes. I think so.'

He was no longer embarrassed to do things naked although in truth the fire was so low as to cast scarcely a glow. He riddled it and added coals, searched for and found his cigarettes. He offered the case to her but she refused.

'No. I don't really like smoking. You smoke a lot, don't you?'

'I could give it up.'

'Could you?'

'I did once. For six months nearly.'

'Why did you start again?

'Someone offered me one at a time when it would have been difficult to refuse.'

'You didn't have to go on.'

'There didn't seem much point in not. In giving it up, I mean. Like when you break a New Year Resolution. You never start all over again, do you?'

When he flicked the lighter he saw her sitting, one of the blankets around her shoulders.

'What time is it?' she said.

'I don't know. I haven't got a watch.'

'I have.' She squinted at her wrist watch but there was insufficient light to read it.

He came over with his case and held the lighter over her. The blanket only covered her shoulders so that it threw shadows of her breasts.

'Half past three,' she said.

'What time will you go?'

'I don't know. Before it gets light.'

'Do you think you'll get away with it?'

'It doesn't matter.'

'I wonder,' he said, 'what we get if we get caught.'

'You'll catch cold. Either get under the blankets or put one round you.'

He was silent for a while, thinking, smoking, and then he said: 'I realise why you came, you know. I'm not a fool.'

'You don't realise at all.'

'Yes, I do. I'm grateful.'

'For God's sake,' she said, 'stop grovelling!'

Her anger surprised but didn't crush him.

'I'm not,' he answered. 'I'm just . . . ' He looked at the upturned beds, at the criss-crossing of the wire bases. 'It was like

310

being in a cage, wasn't it?' he said. 'Did that occur to you?'

'No.'

'It did to me. All the time. It's how I shall always remember it.'

'You don't understand.'

'Yes, I do. I'm not quite a fool.' He pulled one of the blankets off the floor and put it round him and sat hunched with his back to the fire. 'It won't make any difference though,' he said. 'I'm still going to jag it in.'

'No.' She spoke with conviction. 'You won't do that.'

After a while she said: 'Why exactly did I come here then?'

'Out of pity.'

'Out of pity?' She laughed harshly. 'Was what we just did done out of pity?'

'That wasn't why you came. In the first place.'

'Wasn't it?' She pulled the blanket more around her. In the flickering of the resuscitated fire with the blanket round her and her head bent staring past him at the flames she looked witch-like. 'There's only one reason I came,' she told him. 'And that was to have you do what you've just done to me. The rest was just playacting.'

He shook his head. 'I shall never believe that.'

She looked at him. There was still something to be done. 'You know,' she said, 'you're quite a man. Four times already and only halfway through the night. There's not many men who'd be able to match that although a lot of them boast they can. Will you tell them?'

'Tell who what?'

'Tell your chums that Corporal Rivers spent the night with you and how many times you fucked her? And all the other things you did to her and she did to you?'

'Of course I won't.'

'You will, you know. Not right away perhaps. But they'll get to know. One way or another you'll let it out even if its by innuendo or not answering questions. And they'll think the more of you because of it. Just as they will about that first night solo which was quite a performance. You're going to be a character.'

'I give you my word . . . '

'I haven't asked for it. Why shouldn't you give them as good as some of them have been giving you?'

'You wouldn't mind?'

'Well the basics are going to come out, aren't they? Even if I manage to slip out of here without anybody seeing me, you don't imagine my being missing all night's going to

312

go unnoticed do you?'

'They won't have to know that you were here.'

'They'll know I brought you back.'

That was the end of it; there was nothing more to say that wouldn't be repetition.

'Come to bed,' she said. 'You need the rest. You'll be flying again tomorrow.'

★   ★   ★

He was soon asleep but for a long time she stayed awake, watching the fire die down again, listening to the boom of the surf through the thin matchboard walls of the hut. She was sure she had achieved what she had at first told herself she had set out to do; he would awake, shave, dress and go to the mess for breakfast and be at once back with companions engaged in an adventure as exciting as any virile young man could hope for. But with this difference: that he would have come of age. A shift in the flames glinted wires on the base of the upturned bed which barred the door. She remembered what he'd said; that it was like being in a cage. How strange, she thought. For years and years he's been a prisoner of his own self-abnegation and hopefully I've released him; but whether or not I have, there's a price which will have to be paid and we'll be the ones to pay it: Freddie and me. And she thought of what Harry had said about what happened when you broke a New Year resolution — that you didn't go back to trying to keep it afterwards.

We do hope that you have enjoyed reading this large print book.

Did you know that all of our titles are available for purchase?

We publish a wide range of high quality large print books including:
Romances, Mysteries, Classics
General Fiction
Non Fiction and Westerns

Special interest titles available in large print are:
The Little Oxford Dictionary
Music Book
Song Book
Hymn Book
Service Book

Also available from us courtesy of Oxford University Press:
Young Readers' Dictionary
(large print edition)
Young Readers' Thesaurus
(large print edition)

For further information or a free brochure, please contact us at:
Ulverscroft Large Print Books Ltd.,
The Green, Bradgate Road, Anstey,
Leicester, LE7 7FU, England.
Tel: (00 44) 0116 236 4325
Fax: (00 44) 0116 234 0205

STRANGER IN THE PLACE

Anne Doughty

Elizabeth Stewart, a Belfast student and only daughter of hardline Protestant parents, sets out on a study visit to the remote west coast of Ireland. Delighted as she is by the beauty of her new surroundings and the small community which welcomes her, she soon discovers she has more to learn than the details of the old country way of life. She comes to reappraise so much that is slighted and dismissed by her family — not least in regard to herself. But it is her relationship with a much older, Catholic man, Patrick Delargy, which compels her to decide what kind of life she really wants.

RUN WILD MY HEART

Maureen Child

For beautiful Margaret Allen, travelling alone across the western plains was her only escape from a loveless marriage — a marriage secretly arranged by her father as part of a heartless business scheme. In a fury, she left her quiet, unassuming life behind and ventured out on her own ... Cheyenne Boder set out to claim a cash reward for finding Margaret and bringing her home. But the handsome frontiersman found a promise of love in her sweet smile and vowed to unearth the hidden passions that made her a bold, proud woman of the west!

PROUD HEART, FAIR LADY

Elayn Duffy

Viscount Philip Devlin is not a happy man. From his grave, his father has decreed that the Viscount shall marry a girl he has never met if he is to inherit his beloved Meadowsdene and Kingsgrey Court. For a girl with no dowry to speak of, marrying into one of the oldest, richest houses in England is good fortune indeed. But the Viscount's bride, Kathryn Hastings, faces a grim future for she will be his wife in name only, leaving him to pursue his life as before. Kathryn decides to enact her revenge and turns the tables on Devlin.

DUMMY HAND

Susan Moody

When Cassie Swann is knocked off her bike on a quiet country road, the driver leaves her unconscious and bleeding at the roadside. A man later walks into a police station and confesses, and they gratefully close the case. But something about this guilt-induced confession doesn't smell right, and Cassie's relentless suitor Charlie Quartermain cannot resist doing a little detective work. When a young student at Oxford is found brutally murdered, Charlie begins to suspect that the two incidents are somehow connected. Can he save Cassie from another 'accident' — this time a fatal one?

THE SURGEON'S APPRENTICE

Arthur Young

1947: Young Neil Aitken has worked hard to secure a place at Glasgow University to study medicine. Bearing in mind the Dean's warning that it takes more than book-learning to become a doctor, he sets out to discover what that other elusive quality might be. He learns the hard way, from a host of memorable characters ranging from a tyrannical surgeon to the bully on the farm where Neil works in his spare time, and assorted patients who teach him about courage and vulnerability. Neil also meets Sister Annie, the woman who is to influence his life in every way.

1	21	41	61	81	101	121	141	161	181
2	22	42	62	(82)	102	122	142	162	182
3	23	43	63	83	103	123	143	163	183
4	24	44	64	84	104	124	144	164	184
5	25	45	65	85	105	125	145	165	185
6	26	46	66	86	106	126	146	166	186
7	27	47	67	87	107	127	147	167	187
8	28	48	68	88	108	128	148	168	188
9	29	49	69	89	109	129	149	169	189
10	30	50	70	90	110	130	150	170	190
11	31	51	71	91	111	131	151	171	191
12	32	52	72	92	112	132	152	172	192
13	33	53	73	93	113	133	153	173	193
14	34	54	74	94	114	134	154	174	194
15	35	55	75	95	115	135	155	175	195
16	36	56	76	96	116	136	156	176	196
17	37	57	77	97	117	137	157	177	197
18	38	58	78	98	118	138	158	178	198
19	39	59	79	99	119	139	159	179	199
20	40	60	80	100	120	140	160	180	200

201	211	221	231	241	251	261	271	281	291
202	212	222	232	242	252	262	272	282	292
203	213	223	233	243	253	263	273	283	293
204	214	224	234	244	254	264	274	284	294
205	215	225	235	245	255	265	275	285	295
206	216	226	236	246	256	266	276	286	296
207	217	227	237	247	257	267	277	287	297
208	218	228	238	248	258	268	278	(288)	298
209	219	229	239	249	259	269	279	289	299
210	220	230	240	250	260	270	280	290	300

301	310	319	328	337	346
302	311	320	329	338	347
303	312	321	330	339	348
304	313	322	331	(340)	349
305	314	323	332	341	350
306	315	324	333	342	
307	316	325	334	343	
308	317	326	335	344	
309	318	327	(336)	345	